DSI Comegys Library, Walter L. Bicknell

**Sunday Snowdrops**

lay sermons, more especially for the use of young boys

DSI Comegys Library, Walter L. Bicknell

**Sunday Snowdrops**
*lay sermons, more especially for the use of young boys*

ISBN/EAN: 9783337361167

Printed in Europe, USA, Canada, Australia, Japan

Cover: Foto ©Andreas Hilbeck / pixelio.de

More available books at **www.hansebooks.com**

# Sunday Snowdrops.

# LAY SERMONS,

## MORE ESPECIALLY FOR THE USE OF YOUNG BOYS.

BY

## WALTER L. BICKNELL.

LONDON:

J. MASTERS AND CO., 78, NEW BOND STREET.

MDCCCLXXX.

LONDON :

PRINTED BY J. MASTERS AND CO.,

ALBION BUILDINGS, BARTHOLOMEW CLOSE.

DEDICATED TO

ONE

TO WHOM THIS WORK

OWES ITS ORIGIN.

# PREFACE.

THESE few "Sermonettes" do not aim at any pretence of excellence of style, but merely are an effort to place the great truths of religion in as simple and interesting a form as can be for quite young boys. The preparatory school is the nursery of the larger schoolroom, and its children must be fed with "milk." So long as the "milk" is wholesome, and the best of its kind, it sustains and nourishes. If these few feeble words have raised, or will raise any effort after a godly life in the hearts of boys, they will most fully have served their purpose.

I have to acknowledge help to Canon Farrar's "School Sermons," and also to the Rev. C. Darnell, Cargilfield, Edinburgh, for a text on the subject of "The Trinity."

WALTER L. BICKNELL.

*Arden House,*
  *Henley in Arden.*

# CONTENTS.

# SUNDAY SNOWDROPS.

## I.

## HERO WORSHIP.

*"And his servants came near and spake unto him, and said, My father, if the prophet had bid thee do some great thing, wouldest thou not have done it? How much rather then when he saith to thee, Wash, and be clean."*—2 Kings v. 13.

You probably all know something about the story from which these words of my text are taken. Naaman the Syrian was a mighty man, and the chief man in the kingdom of Syria: but he was a leper. It happened that a little maid had been captured by the Syrians, and brought away from her home far away in Israel to serve in Naaman's house. This little maid waited on Naaman's wife, and in her eager zeal to do some good to her master she told her mistress of a man of GOD in her own land of Israel who could heal even such a disease as leprosy. Naaman, hearing of this, went

B

in great state with his chariot, horses, and atten-
dants, and stood at the door of the house of Elisha
the prophet of Israel.   Naaman thought that the
prophet would at once come down to such a great
man as he was, and heal him at once by some
wonderful means.   Surely such a great man as the
captain of the host of Syria would not be cured in
any common way.   But Naaman was disappointed.
For the prophet Elisha did not come down himself, but only sent a messenger, who bade him go
and wash seven times in the river Jordan.   Go
and wash seven times in Jordan !   And to be told
this through a messenger !   The pride of Naaman
could not put up with such treatment.   He turned
away in anger.   "Why should I wash in Jordan?"
said he ; " are there not in my own land of Syria
such rivers as Abana and Pharpar? may I not
wash in them, and be cleansed from this leprosy?"

Now, if Naaman had gone home again and not
done the simple bidding of the prophet, as far as
we know, he would never have been cured.   But
his servants were wiser than their master.   They
came up to Naaman—and he must have been a
kind master for them to dare to take such open
interest in his welfare—and said to him the words
of my text.   What they said in effect was this.
"If Elisha had bidden you go and do some great
thing, you would have been willing to do it; but
you don't like doing such a mere simple act as
washing in the little river of Jordan."   And God

willed that Naaman should listen to their wise advice—go and wash in the river, and be cleansed of his leprosy.

Now the lesson which I wish you to carry away with you to-night, and to put in practice during this and all weeks, is one which we all take much time to learn, and many times forget. We so often wish to be heroes. We think it a grand thing to be a hero, to do or say something out of the common. Our life here seems often dull, perhaps wearisome and very tame. We seem to have no great opportunities for doing any really great and noble act. Let me ask you then whom you think a hero? and I ask you this, because sometimes the world calls those heroes who are not, and sometimes does not call those heroes who are such in the best and truest sense.

Now I take it, we all from our youngest days have had some hero, whom we have known, and if not known, admired at a distance. It may be a father, a brother, a friend. We all more or less make a hero of our father. In our infancy we think there is no one so great, so strong, so noble as our father. Years go by, and we perhaps find a new hero in a schoolfellow who is clever, or strong, or popular; or in some one who attracts us, and whom we imitate in our daily life. I regret to have to say, our hero worship, our Dagon, is far too often dashed to earth with older years. Could you but lift the veil and peep into your hero's heart ; could you but snatch the mask from his face, you would sometimes find that he is not the hero he seems, that he has many and serious flaws and faults.    Perhaps (though you are now too young to understand at least fully its meaning) there are few moments in our life so full of present anguish, so fraught with a sense of uncertainty, helplessness, and doubt of all that is good and noble—as when some one in whom we rested most absolute repose of trust, one whom we admired deeply and loved, falls into grievous sin, and is dashed from the pedestal where we at least in fancy had placed him or her.    For a moment our belief in goodness is terribly shaken, and we seem as startled suddenly and rudely out of a dream in which we would still wish to linger on.

> " What reed was that on which I leant ?
> Ah ! backward, fancy, wherefore wake
> The old bitterness again, and break
> The low beginnings of content ?"

The world has its heroes, and it may be that its heroes are at times noble and virtuous.    Who but admires the boy Casabianca, as he stands on the burning deck, dying for duty and obedient to his father's word?    Who of us does not love the picture of Grace Darling rowing out herself amid the wild waves to save the lives that but for her help had perished?    And cold must be our hearts, if they do not thrill at such noble actions as those lately done by those two gallant young lieutenants in that distant war in South Africa, who lost their lives in the daring attempt to recover the colours of their regiments? Such was the valour that sent the gallant Six Hundred "into the jaws of death, into the mouth of hell." Yes, to be sure, these actions one and all are noble, and the actions of heroes. Yet there are heroes and heroines whose *lives* have been more noble, more heroic, than the *deaths* even of these heroes. For, though it seems strange, and may be untrue to you, to live is sometimes harder than to die. To live a life of active work, to present a smiling face when the heart aches with a deep hidden sorrow, to forget what *might have been* in what *is*,—this is, believe me, a task that requires a true heroic heart, a task that were too much for us away from GOD's inward peace and sustaining comfort. Let me shortly tell you this evening of three heroic lives, and if their authors have conquered no nations, won no mighty victories, been no mighty actors on this world's stage, I leave their lives before you to speak for themselves.

And I will venture to select my first heroic life from a story which perhaps some of you have read. It is the story of a little girl, who was born of no high rank, and had no advantages of birth or education, but who was a heroine, if I mistake not. She was afraid that her grandfather, an old man of weak mind, would be torn from her, and be given up to cruel hands. Quite a child, she left her

home with him, and wandered far and wide through
the green lanes of old England—past quiet churchyards and peaceful villages, amid the smoke and
dust, and heat of crowded cities—until after many
sufferings and every care of her grandfather, she
brought him to a happy home in the country, where
he might pass his happy days in peace, until a
quiet death should release him.   But the child had
overtaxed her little strength.   Her mission on
earth was done, and she passed herself away, tired
and footsore from her weary wandering, into that
land where the weary are at rest.   Believe me,
that little girl lying there in that quiet country
churchyard, loved by many a heart both young
and old, is a heroine; and her name is little Nell.

And my second hero is no one known to fame.
Merely an old man living in a garret high up in an
old German town.   He is poor and alone, and
with no one to care for or love him.   Not a very
interesting hero this, you think.   He was a mighty
painter, yet, though now an old man, he had not
gained fame for his pictures, for the world denied
that his paintings were great and worthy of reward.
And at this time there was a great prize given in
the town for the best picture that could be sent in
to the judges.   As it chanced, a young artist who
was sending in a picture fought a duel, and was
carried to his own lodging well-nigh dead.   No
one came to help him there but this old man, who
sat by his bedside and nursed him in his long hours

of delirium when he knew nothing. And there was his unfinished picture on the easel. The old man looked on it, and saw that it was weak and unworthy of the prize or of fame : and he worked himself and fashioned a noble picture that should be praised through all time. Then he sent this in as the sick young artist's handiwork. It won the prize easily, and the young man arose from his sick bed to be famous far and wide. The old man stole back to his garret, to die, and I venture to call that old man a hero.

But I have yet another hero to tell you of, and one very very far removed from any I have yet spoken of—yet one poor, despised, scoffed at, and at last put to a shameful death. He left His Father's home in heaven to live a life on earth of poverty and sorrow. He was tempted, He was sorely tried by bitter foes, and worse by the desertion of trusted friends. He drank the bitter cup of anguish to the dregs, and even GOD hid His face from His soul, and a moment of unspeakable loneliness fell upon Him, wringing from Him the cry, " My GOD, My GOD, why hast Thou forsaken Me ?" To the eye of the world this was no hero's life. Where was the world's applause ? Where was the glory, the glitter, the pleasure of such a life ? Yet

> " Is it so small a thing
> To have lived—to have wrought—to have done ?"

And that life which must have seemed to many

painful, unfruitful, useless, a life of unceasing self-sacrifice and unselfishness, and taking on Himself the sins of the whole world, that life was that of the greatest Hero that ever walked on this earth of ours—and His name was JESUS CHRIST.

But, boys, many of you think, I dare say, This last hero is too far above me. The greatness and goodness of JESUS CHRIST is out of my reach. I cannot attain unto it. And for the rest, you do not see how you can ever be like the heroes in your daily life at school and at home. But be certain that

> " Day by day each Christian child
> Has much to do without, within."

And before I leave off speaking to you to-night I will very briefly tell you how I think you all, even to the very youngest here, may be heroes in the best sense of the word. And I will only name two ways to you : first, to do your duty where you are ; second, to forget self. First, don't say, If I was in such and such a position, I could act rightly. Don't lay the fault on any one but yourself. GOD has made you what you each are ; and He has given to each one of you his own work to do. Don't leave your work, and try to do some one else's which seems to suit you better. Whatever your station in life, do your duty, and then you will be a true hero. Good intentions, strong emotion, good feeling, are most valuable ; but if all

the while you shirk your duty and neglect what
you ought to do, you can be no hero. There is a
republic of heroism. I mean that the poorest
ragged boy in the slums and alleys of our great
cities, and the most miserable men and women
may be true heroes, and with this much more
credit to them, that their opportunities are less
and their knowledge of good ofttimes dim. No,
we must all accept the duty before us, and do it,
however hard and irksome it seems, and make
drudgery divine and the meanest act noble. So
we raise our duty. And second, we must take up
our cross, and follow CHRIST. We must deny
ourselves, and forget ourselves in others. You
will say this is very hard. Yes, it is hard, the
hardest lesson any of us can learn; for we are so
bound up in ourselves that it seems impossible
that we should not all our lives be striving and
struggling for our own success. Yet he is no true
hero who puts self first. When any of you pushes
away the cloud of ill feeling and sullenness which
is beginning to steal across his heart; when any of
you is not ashamed of CHRIST before men, i.e.
when you are tempted by others to wrong and you
refuse, or when you boldly declare that this or that
act is wrong and all ought to turn away from it.
Then, believe me, then you are acting the part of
a hero. The true hero is manly, and he is not
ashamed of his better feelings : he is not ashamed
of his home affections, his love for dear ones who

have cared for him, his love for what is good and pure and virtuous. And he who is no hero is unmanly, and is ashamed of these high and purifying feelings which GOD hath put into well-nigh every heart,—nay, I say all hearts. Those of you who go hence into a large public school may remember these feeble words of mine,—for you will find, I fear, those there often who think little of evil and speak lightly of what is wrong. If you value your own happiness, if you would preserve your soul pure and unspotted from the world, think of these words, or rather think of those far more awful words of CHRIST, " Of him that is ashamed of Me before men, will I be ashamed in the kingdom of My FATHER." Therefore I beg you most earnestly, as you are where GOD has placed you, try and put self away and think of others, and as you can do neither without GOD's help, pray to Him to make you think little of yourself, much of others, to do good honest work for GOD in this life; and so will you find a new meaning in your week-day life, in every little act you do; you will be growing more like a manly, unselfish, GOD-fearing hero. And do you ask where?

> " The trivial round, the common task,
> Will furnish all we need to ask,
> Room to deny ourselves, a road
> To bring us daily nearer GOD."

## II.

## WATCHFULNESS.

*"Watch and pray."*—S. Matt. xxvi. 41.

IT is morning, and the sun shines brightly down upon the vast castle and its princely gardens which stretch sloping away as far as the eye can reach. Up and down the walks, along the parapets of the castle, alike inside the halls and outside, rings the sound of gay revelry and glad rejoicing. Bands of revellers hasten hither and thither, forming plans of happiness for to-day or for the morrow. The scene is one of busy eager happiness. And yet here and there are those who seem anxious and well-nigh fearful, as of some coming evil, bright though the sky is, and distant as seems even the suspicion of danger. Danger! where can danger be amid these bands of happy men and women and children, among flowers of fairest hue, and encircled as all are on every side by objects of gaiety and loveliness? Yet there is mistrust and anxiety written on the brows of not a few: and others, though with no appearance of dread, but with a quiet trustful look are watching intensely as though in the far horizon some object were to be seen. And I looked, and saw nothing.

And there were two sitting on the old ivy-clad

battlement, watching with an intense gaze,—one an old man with long white hair, and the other a young child, holding the old man's hand in his own. And I touched the old man and said,

"Why do you two sit here idly watching instead of being gay as are all the others? Why so sad in the midst of rejoicing?"

And I saw a tear gather in his eye, yet he smiled and said, "O sir, say not so; I am happy, yes, even though an old pilgrim, I can look back with happiness on the days that have been. I am not sad,—oh no. But my dear Master, Whose is this castle, and Whose servant I am, has bidden us watch and look for His chariot, as He will come driving over yonder hills in the dim horizon."

And I said, "But this child, must he sit here? Surely children such as he should be gay and enjoy themselves?"

And the child smiled also, and looked up in the old man's face. "O sir," said the child, "I am very happy, and do not think I am sad. But I am likewise our great Master's servant, and He has been so good and kind to us all, should we not do what He wishes? And oh! I do so long to see His face; and I know He loves the little children."

And then I saw the badge of their belonging to this great Lord, and it was a cross on their foreheads—very plain and easy to be seen in both, though but lately set upon the little one.

Yes, and all the revellers, every one, I saw wore this badge, though some had such a very faint one that it was almost lost altogether, and many seemed ashamed of it.

So the afternoon wore on—hot and sultry, and a gentle breeze arose about eventide. Then the revellers sat them down to a great feast, and loud and long was the shouting and gaiety of the feasters. Still these two watched on, and so did a few others, though ever and anon one here and there would leave the task of watching and take their place at the board. And yet even some of those feasting now and then started and looked round in fear: and first one or two stole away amid the jeers of the others to take their place among the silent watchers.

So night came. The feast has ended, and the revellers have betaken them to their slumbers. And it was in the cool hour before dawn, just the brief hour ere the world wakes to labour,—when lo, the great Master came. Why knew not all of it? Is it not ever true—

> " The night is darkest before the dawn,
>  When the pain is sorest the child is born,
>  And the day of the LORD is at hand ?"

He came in silence over the distant hills, and His horses were fleet as the wings of the wind. Yet not a man, woman, or child, but started to their feet in the silence; and the cry arose, "Go ye out to

meet Him." O the ang
those revellers ! How th
robes of feasting and c
sought to remove the stair
their garments. All, all
ready.

Useless their cry,

"Have we not heard the l'
O let us in, that we may

Nay, ever on the winds wa
tive whispering, now ebbi
late ! too late ! ye cannot c

And those who had wat
them ? I know not, for
from my eyes; only for o
catch sight of the beaut
upon the face of the gre
upon that old man and the
them in His arms, not as
loved children. And they

Now, boys, there is on
beg you most clearly to
ceed to apply this allegory
cuss the meaning of the
that is, Don't think that to
of all joy and happiness,
thing sad and gloomy. N
Theirs is the deepest and
ever bear in their hearts

in their h

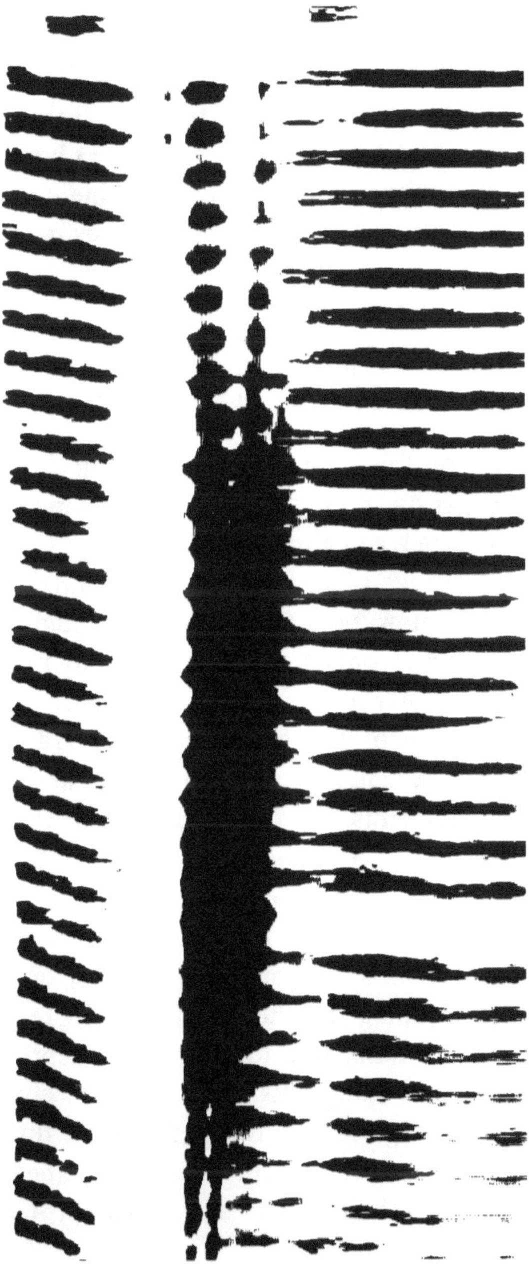

meet Him." O the anguish and awful dread of
those revellers! How they tried to tear off the
robes of feasting and drunkenness; how they
sought to remove the stains of the wine cup from
their garments. All, all in vain,—they were not
ready.

Useless their cry,

> "Have we not heard the Bridegroom is so sweet?
>   O let us in, that we may kiss His feet."

Nay, ever on the winds was borne along the plain-
tive whispering, now ebbing, now swelling, "Too
late! too late! ye cannot enter now!"

And those who had watched,—how fared it with
them? I know not, for they were caught away
from my eyes; only for one brief moment did I
catch sight of the beauteous smile that dawned
upon the face of the great Master as He looked
upon that old man and the little child, and folded
them in His arms, not as servants, but as dearly
loved children. And they were lost to sight.

Now, boys, there is one thing which I would
beg you most clearly to understand ere we proceed to apply this allegory to ourselves, or to discuss the meaning of the words of the text, and
that is, Don't think that to *watch* will deprive you
of all joy and happiness, that it is merely something sad and gloomy. No, a thousand times *no*.
Theirs is the deepest and truest happiness who
ever bear in their hearts the voice of CHRIST,

"Behold I stand at the door and knock," yet who go about their daily duties in life, and take alike the daily happiness and daily toil of life, not in melancholy sort, not with the sad face of the Pharisee, but serving GOD cheerfully, and doing their duty to their fellows, only keeping their best and intensest affection for their GOD, their SAVIOUR, their Comforter, in Whose bosom there ever remaineth a rest for the people of GOD.

The text says,—Watch. And you will perhaps say, How can I watch? Watch in thought, watch in word, watch in act.

*In thought.* For the true knight cannot even think treason, and Satan is ever ready to cast his darts through the loopholes of our thoughts, if we allow a single chink to be in the very least open. In the times of our leisure, when we are not safe in active employment, when a rush of diverse thought comes sweeping over our souls as the wind across the waves of grass,—in such times when the soul is empty of action, Satan steals upon us. The house of the soul must be at times void of a tenant, either good or evil. See to it that it be quickly filled by the Spirit of GOD; see to it that holy influences nestle there and surround it on every side; see to it that nothing impure, foolish, or unholy, breathe in those hallowed precincts. Does a boy here ever murmur in thought at some rule which to him seems hard? does he feel envy of another's greater talent and strength of body or mind? does he feel conceited, and though wearing outwardly pretence of modesty, secretly be vainly puffed up as though his knowledge or power were of any account? Watch such thoughts, for they are the tares of Satan; and if you once admit them, they will multiply and beget evil words and evil acts. Man may not see them, but ever remember, "Thou GOD seest me!"

And again, *in word.* Watch. Watch, for here is the devil busy hourly, ay, every minute of our lives. Most awful is the responsibility of words,—for has not CHRIST Himself said, "By thy words thou shalt be justified," i.e., saved; "and by thy words thou shalt be condemned?" And yet again, "every idle word that men shall speak, they shall give account of in the day of judgment." Take the words of each day,—from early morn till the moment when you lie down, would there be no word of unkindness, of ill-temper, of malice, of deceit, of impurity, of peevishness? I fear not one or two, but *many.* Therefore I say to you, watch over your words.

Perhaps they seem to you mere empty sounds, meaning little or nothing; but they ofttimes wound, ofttimes hide the truth, ofttimes offend "GOD Who is Love!" You discuss some one's character, you pick out his peculiarities, his weaknesses, his failings, his faults. Why should you not rather be silent on them, and if you cannot praise, do not find fault. Do you not often seek to create a

laugh by detailing some story to the discredit or
ridicule of another? Throw away your vanity which
makes you tell the story, and leave the story
untold.

And yet once more, *in your acts*. Watch.
Never think yourselves safe, no, rather, " Let him
that thinketh he standeth take heed lest he fall."
In your humility lies your strength, in your conceit
lies your weakness. The boy who thinks himself
strong enough to resist temptation, who is "wise
in his own conceits," who thinks himself clever,
and better than others in his heart,—of such an
one the wisest of men sharply and sternly says,
" There is more hope of a fool than of him." That
boy is an easy prey to Satan, for he is standing on
the verge of a steep precipice of which he knows
nothing. Far rather is he likely to be safe who
distrusts himself, who is modest, unassuming, not
puffed up by self-esteem; who does not value the
worthless praise of unthinking persons, who feeling his own weakness, is ever watchful against
temptation. Therefore I earnestly beg, in *thought*,
*word*, and *deed*, ever be on your watch. Avoid
any companions, any situation, any place, where it
is difficult to you to watch, where temptation most
easily assails you.

And here must follow the second half of the text,
—not only " *watch*," but "*pray*." For how can the
true soldier of JESUS CHRIST watch aright, unless
he be armed with the mail armour of "*prayer* ?"

C

There are souls which are so girt round with the
spirit of prayer, that they indeed walk with GOD,
and are ever with the LORD.

> "Thrice blest whose lives are faithful prayers,
>   Whose loves in higher loves endure ;
>   What souls possess themselves so pure,
>   Or is there blessedness like theirs ?"

To-night, in the few minutes that remain, I
would try to show you, (1) The power of prayer,
(2) The sympathy of prayer.  And I cannot here
for lack of time speak of the deep importance of
public prayer, but only of those petitions which
you send up all of you, I trust, night and morning
to GOD, those darts of prayer wherewith you do
most grievously wound Satan and pierce even the
throne of GOD Himself.  I say then, such prayer is
all-powerful.  It is all-powerful against Satan, for
he cannot assail the child of GOD when he is on
his knees in the presence-chamber of his FATHER
in heaven.  No attitude is so hopeless to the
Devil and his wiles as that of prayer.  And is it
not true that

> "More things are wrought by prayer
>   Than this world dreams of ?"

Not to speak of the power of public prayer, of
the pleading of a whole nation with GOD, as perhaps some of you remember when England's
prayers rose up for our Prince well-nigh on the

bed of death : are there not many times in our
lives when we feel that prayer can alone avail?
We have requests which we make to GOD for ourselves, let us pray in faith that He will give them
if good for us,—and if not, "His will be done."
Let us wrestle all night with Him and prevail over
Him by our might of prayerful energy. And not
only for ourselves, but for others,—shall we not
pray for our dear and near ones,—those whose
weal or woe is bound up in ours, be they far or
near; for the whole brotherhood of mankind, ay,
and for those who cause us pain. Shall not the
father and mother pray for their dear one far
away from home, far from the shelter and tenderness of love? shall they not kneel by the empty
bedside where in infancy and boyhood their dear
one lay, and supplicate in secret their FATHER
above to turn the heart of that wayward child,
exiled from home, and lead him by words of love
to a mother's embrace and a father's blessing.
And yet one step more. Is not prayer able to lift
the veil of death for us, and carry us for a little
while out of the struggling day of life into the
bright communion of saints, and let us hear for a
moment the melody of the angels singing round
the great white throne?

And lastly. Has prayer no sympathy in its right
hand? They best know who put it to the test.
In this world we are ever at times *alone*. The
friends of our whole life, those who are intimately

bound up in our lives, they deem they know us,—
but do they? Have we not got deep down in the
hiding-place of our hearts a hope, a struggle, a
disappointment, a yearning, with which a stranger,
(nay more, the dearest friend,) cannot intermeddle? We bar the entrance to such with a jealous
care; we will not that any should enter that
"study" of thought known and felt alone by us.
Here and there in our lives we retire there and
ponder over the shelves of thoughts laid aside,
hopes, bright enough once, but now laden with the
dust of hard fact and reality; disappointments
hidden from the eye of the world, but to which we
can turn from page to page with exact memory.
Passing words, shot out at random, may make us
fly thither; here a memory, there a memory may
knock at its door,—GOD alone shares the full
knowledge.

> "There is a secret place of rest,
> 　　GOD's saints alone may know,
> Thou shalt not find it east or west,
> 　　Though seeking to and fro;
> A cell where JESUS is the door,
> 　　His love the only key;
> Who enter will go out no more,
> 　　But there with JESUS be."

Yes, my dear boys, bear these words of our
LORD JESUS CHRIST ever with you. In prayer and
humble watchfulness you have an unceasing safety.
For if here on earth you have from your boyhood

upwards kept your eyes fixed not on the prizes of
the world, not on self, not on mere earthly success,
but on that far off land where your heart and treasure should be; if you have never forgotten that
prayer is the only road whereby the Christian
traveller can walk securely,—then will you, one
and all, come to that dear home where watching
shall be lost in the everlasting presence of God
Himself, and the tearful pleadings of prayer be
merged into praise and the song of triumph. To
which may God, for His dear Son's sake, bring us
every one.

## III.

### CHRISTIAN HEALTH.

*" Is it well with the child? It is well."*—2 Kings iv. 26.
*" I say unto you, that in heaven their angels do always be-
hold the face of My Father Which is in heaven."*—S. Matt.
xviii. 10.

It was a fair and lovely garden wherein I stood.
The flowers were of the fairest hues, and as the
morning sun rose in all his beauty and drew up
into his hand the misty dews which were spread
as a curtain before the face of the earth, each
flower arose, and smiled to see the face of day re-

turning once more to gladden nature with his sunny smile. And I looked, and behold, there were four beds of flowers, and in one bed were snowdrops; in a second, were hyacinths; in a third, roses; and in the fourth, white lilies. And presently the gardener came forth into the garden; and I saw him that he was about to gather a nosegay. And he paused long, and looked carefully at the four beds. And I know not why, but there came across my mind the words of a Book wherein I was wont to read, and the words were, "My Beloved is gone down into His garden to gather lilies." And I said to him, "O sir, must you pick any of these flowers, and what mean these four beds?" And he said with a smile that broke like the rising sun across his grave and beautiful face, "These four beds it is my fancy to call Spring, Summer, Autumn, and Winter, and every morning I come into my garden, and therein I pick out such flowers as seem to me the meetest and choicest out of these four beds. And as to your question whether I cannot let them alone, I cannot, for though your eye may not discern the need, these flowers I am now choosing are ripe and ready for my hand." And I said, "At least, sir, spare these snowdrops so white and pure; spare them a little longer, to gladden my eyes." And I saw a tear gather in his eye, and he said, "You ask me a hard thing, but I cannot spare even these. I love them of all flowers the most dearly,

and I must take them to myself." And I saw that
he laid them with most tender care in his arms,
and with especial watchfulness lest they should
take harm, and I know not how it was, but once
more the words of that favourite Book of mine
came before me. "He gathereth the lambs into
His bosom, and tenderly leadeth those that are
with young." And yet again, "He is thy refuge,
and underneath are the everlasting arms." And
even as I mused on these old old words, the gardener and the garden slowly vanished from my
eyes. I awoke, and behold it was a dream.

Now, boys, in this allegory or story, weak and
badly expressed, as I doubt not it is, I would have
you read the answer to my question of the text,
"Is it well with the child? *It is well.*" These
words carry us back to the Shunammite woman and
her son, of whom it is said, "He sat on her knees
till noon, and then died." There she sits and looks
out of the open door upon the reapers, among
whom the father of the lad is working amid the
yellow corn. The sun shines very hotly, men pass
and repass, the busy work of reaping never flags;
all looks the same as yesterday; ay, but a new
reaper has entered that field, a reaper whose name
is Death. There sits on the mother, and in the
sanctuary of her heart she communes alone with a
grief that cries with Joseph, "Cause every man to
go out from me." She had seen her boy start
gaily forth, holding his father's hand, and waving

his little hand to her as she stood looking at their
retreating figures in the door of the tent.   She
sits on, stunned; the waves of sorrow come rushing over her soul, unable to reason, to think, even
to dare to think.   Yet, mother, take courage, GOD
has comfort in store for thee.

> " Thy little child has gone to sleep,
>     Why should'st thou, mother, watch and weep?
>     Earth's ills were gathering round his nest,
>     He crept into a FATHER'S breast."

Boys, the first question I ask you to-night is,
" Is it well with *you now ?*   Is it well with you in
*this life ?*"   For, if you can answer from your heart,
" It is well," it, must be well with you hereafter.
And if you say, " How can I tell if ' it is well' with
me now? what examination can I put to myself?
how can I feel the pulse of every thought, word,
and deed, of my life?"   I would say, Examine
yourselves and your actions carefully, if not each
night, at least often; prove the ground of your
own hearts to see if there be any wickedness in
you.   You, each of you, here before me to-night,
know your own besetting sins.   You know in your
heart of hearts that you are a hypocrite—not in-
tentionally so, GOD forbid I should say so—but
none the less a hypocrite.   You work well, you
play well, you succeed, and are getting on ; your
masters speak well of you ; your father and mother
give a good report of you.   You mean to do

well, when surrounded by good influences, you feel
strongly moved to good at times. Yet all the
time you feel your heart is not with GOD, and
seeking the things of GOD. You have no root,
and in time of temptation, in after life, you will
fall away. "Let him that thinketh he standeth,
take heed lest he fall." You know well that you
are given not to speak the exact truth—to hide
back part, for fear of punishment, for fear of being
thought less well of. Or, again, you know that
you are given to exaggerate, to make things out
different and more grand than they really are, to
say what makes you seem somebody of importance,
and to give the impression that you have taken a
prominent share in, or have done something in,
what you took little or no part in. Or, it may be,
you dislike not having the best things for yourself;
you have from long habits of thinking only of
yourself, strangely forgotten those around you. A
pleasure is proposed, a game is started, a gratifica-
tion is to be enjoyed, your only thought is, "What
shall *I* have in all this? how soon may *I* take part
in all this pleasure?" You have not learned the
lesson, Deny thyself, and follow CHRIST, take up
the Cross daily—daily, yes, in little kindnesses,
unseen by any eye save GOD's. Daily, yes, in
little acts of giving up some thing you like, that
another may have it. Daily, yes, in a kind word
or action to some one you don't care much about,
and perhaps rather look down upon. Or, lastly,

you cannot always govern your temper. You show vexation at little mishaps, you are peevish, and inclined to be sulky, because of little failures and disappointments, and you dislike reproof and kindly advice, and only regard such as a nuisance—something to be avoided, or at least to be got over as soon as may be.

I say, then, Examine yourselves on each and all of these. Are you overcoming such faults? or are they growing upon you? The tares must grow stronger and quicker than the wheat, if you do not root them up. In your humility lies your strength. Think humbly of yourselves; forget yourselves in others, and in GOD's work; and pray night and morning to GOD, Who alone can give you that peace which the world cannot give, to grant you a new heart, a conquest over these besetting sins, grace to be better, and more closely with Him. By such a conquest of self, by such a victory over your everyday temptations alike of school life and home life; by such acts of kindness to those around you, you will be doing *angel's work* below, and in answer to the question, " Is it well with the child?" we may hopefully say, " It is well."

Well, then, secondly, and lastly, so living the life of an angel on earth, you will at length come to be among the number of those who always behold the face of our FATHER Which is in Heaven. GOD may call you away at any time. The great Gardener of the garden of life may shed a tear

more over the snowdrop of life's spring-time, more
over the pure soul just opening its eyes to the
sunshine of this world, than over the rose which
has felt the heat and burden of the day, and has
reached the yellow autumn-tide, or even the dreary
winter of life. But He pauses not, He plucks the
snowdrop, yes, and bids us dry our tears, and be
troubled not at His jealous care, which will keep
these tender nurslings lost to us, safe in His
bosom : for thus parted from us, they are ever with
the LORD. Could you but peep through the veil
of death, would you not see a countless number of
children clothed in white robes, ever singing joy-
fully before the Throne? Think you not that *He*
takes special delight in their infant songs of praise
Who hath said, "Suffer the little children to come
unto Me, for of such is the kingdom of Heaven ?"

Why were they taken from us ? Why was that
young voice, so full of fresh strong life, so soon
hushed ? Why were they snatched hence, just beginning to try their wings and thinking of a bolder flight
through the air, when GOD called them? These have
but alighted in this world, and taken one look around,
a look too pure and innocent to behold aught of
evil, and then flown hence, only to revisit this
earth as blessed spirits, longing to comfort sorrow-
ing dear ones here below, yet full of joy, and ever
looking in their Heavenly FATHER's face. Should
we weep sore for them ? should we mourn as those
without hope ? No, oh surely no. Here we have

had but one fond embrace. Here we had kissed that young cheek but once. Here we but taught them to lisp at our knee " Our FATHER." They have finished the prayer in Heaven, in their FATHER'S presence; they have been enfolded in GOD's arms. And you shall yet again behold them, in that far-off land, pure, sinless, and unbespattered by the mud with which we poor weary pilgrims have been covered in our footsore, uphill journey through life. Perchance had they lived, evil might have befallen them by the way. Those lips might have learned to utter words foul and hateful to the hearing of the all-pure and holy GOD. Those little hands might have wrought deeds of violence; that young soul might have been sadly stained by the pollution of sin. We are spared from such foreboding, for they are with GOD *Who gave them.* GOD gave us these bright jewels, these snowdrops, in His mercy; He hath taken them back to Himself; He has but received His own gift. "The LORD gave, and the LORD hath taken away; blessed be the Name of the LORD."

Therefore, my dear boys, remember now so to walk as to be always ready. Remember, that according as you do angel's work here below, will you see your FATHER's Face, and stand with that bright band in Heaven, and so living, come your Master's call in your boyhood or in old age, we may say of you with a good hope, " *It is well with the child.*"

" They are going, only going,
    JESUS called them long ago,
All the wintry time they're passing
    Softly as the falling snow.
When the violets in the spring time
    Catch the azure of the sky,
They are carried out to slumber
    Sweetly where the violets lie.

" Little hearts for ever stainless,
    Little hands as pure as they,
Little feet, by angels guided
    Never a forbidden way,
They are going, ever going,
    Leaving many a lonely spot,
But 'tis JESUS Who has called them,
    Suffer and forbid them not."
                        *Lyra Apostolica.*

## IV.

## WORK'S BLESSING.

"*Man goeth forth to his work and to his labour until the evening.*"—Ps. civ. 23.

THE command to labour is made holy to us by
the Word of GOD Himself, Who laid this law of
work on Adam, and through him on the whole
human race. The curse on man was, seen aright,
a blessing. " In the sweat of thy brow shalt thou
eat bread till thou return unto the earth." And

again, the SON of GOD says of Himself and His
FATHER, "My FATHER worketh hitherto, and I
work."

Since the days of Adam it has been appointed
to man to work. At the first men dwelt in tents,
and were shepherds. They had large flocks, which
they tended, dwelling in the plains, as we read of
Abraham and Isaac, and the patriarchs of old.
This was the life of the family, the earliest collection of human existence. But from a gathering
together of families rose the village, later the town.
Man's wants began to increase with increase of
land and increase of numbers. The little plot
which sufficed for the father was not enough for
the sons. One man began to covet the land of
his neighbour, and sought to make it his own.
Jealousy and evil passions provoked strife and war,
and war required arms. The owner of the soil
called for weapons, and his demand had to be met
with a supply. Thus arose at once a large trade.
But little by little as the lord, by his superior strength
or mind, became far greater than the folk under
him, he conceived a desire for hitherto unknown
luxuries. Thus arose a trade which ministered to
the pleasure of the lords and masters of the earth,
so society, the life of man with his fellows on earth
became more complicated, as wants, or at least re-
quirements, increased. In the history of the world
we find the power of strength and courage long
prevailing. The knight with his mail armour, his

powerful horse, his noble bearing, is the central
figure, and military service and skill in war is
ranked in the foremost place. We are moved by
the thrilling epic of Rome, which begins, "Arma
virumque cano." "Of arms and the chief I sing,"
says the poet Virgil. We dwell with delight on
the "doughty deeds" of Achilles, the Greek chief
before Troy, or the manly courage of Hector, the
still grander champion of Troy. Richard Cœur
de Lion is the hero of our childhood, as he smites
down the Saracens in the Holy Land, and breaks
through ranks of his retreating foes with his "red
right hand" and his trusty battle-axe. But in our
day, as a very great writer, Carlyle, has said well,
"The true epic of our times is, not *arms and the
man;* but *tools and the man.*" The poetry, fancy,
gleam, of knighthood, and the warrior's life, have
given way to the more prosaic daily work of manu-
facture, and the hammer of Nasmyth, the engineer-
ing of Stephenson and Brunel, the machinery of
Whitworth.

But even from the days when Adam all alone
first began to till the soil to the present hour, when
millions of men and women are earning daily bread
by the sweat of their brow, the voice of history has
repeated the Voice of GOD, " Man goeth forth to
.his work and to his labour until the evening."

Let us first briefly look at CHRIST's life on earth,
our perfect pattern. He has hallowed the life of
business, and the life of retirement, alike in His

own person. A friend of publicans and sinners,
He trod the dusty streets of Jerusalem, frequented
the temple, and the places where men mostly do
congregate. He was reproached by the Pharisees
as "a man gluttonous and a wine-bibber," and at
the same time He was left alone on the mountain
top praying to His GOD and His FATHER. He
ever and anon withdrew Himself from His disciples to some lone place apart, and in the last
agony in the quiet garden of Gethsemane, He
poured out His soul to GOD alone, and away even
from His chosen three disciples. Yes, and GOD
too (if we may say so) alike works and rests.
During the six days of the life of this world GOD
ever works for the welfare and good of man. He,
the Almighty FATHER, ever works good for us His
children : till that great seventh day, that never
ending Sabbath come, bringing an everlasting day
of rest alike to GOD, and the people of GOD.

So then it seems that our life ought to consist
of seasons of repose, and seasons of work. First,
then, as to repose ; it is necessary to bring work to
perfection in everything. In the bustle and hurry
of life the great man steps aside to think : it is
from his study or studio that the masterpieces of
art and genius go forth to dazzle the world. Turner,
one of the greatest, if not the greatest, nature
painter of the world, spent hours simply in looking
on nature, without using his pencil at all. It is
said of him that he was seen to spend a whole day,

sitting upon a rock and throwing pebbles into a
lake; and when at evening his fellow-painters
showed their day's sketches and rather laughed at
him for having done nothing, he answered, "I
have done this at least, I have learnt how a lake
looks when pebbles are thrown into it." Sir Joshua
Reynolds, another famous painter, when once
asked how long it had taken him to paint a certain
picture, replied, "*All my life.*" And surely if this
silent labour and fixed attention are required by
the painter, are they not required likewise by the
seeker after GOD? How can we ever learn "the
mysteries of GOD" and muse in silent thought on
the problems of life and eternity, if we do not set
apart rare intervals of spiritual leisure and of close
communion with GOD and the things of GOD?

But, to-night, I rather wish to dwell for a few
moments on the grandeur and the blessing of work.
And I would first say, Never fall into the idea
that work is unnecessary for success, that you need
not work to attain a good name, that true genius
*nascitur non fit,* i.e. is born, and does not rather
grow step by step. Here and there in the world's
history, there have been geniuses, whose fame has
shone across the sky like a meteor, dazzling bright,
but only gleaming for an instant, and then vanish-
ing into darkness. But such men may be counted
on your fingers. For not even men the most
famous and renowned have laid aside work or
neglected hard study. Let me give you an in-

stance from the life of a wellknown novelist and
poet.  " He made it a rule to answer every letter
(sometimes amounting to 100) on the same day.
It was his practice to rise by five o'clock, and light
his own fire.  By six o'clock he was seated at his
desk, with his papers arranged before him in the
most perfect order.  Thus, by the time the family
assembled for breakfast, between nine and ten, he
had done enough to break the neck of the day's
work.  Yet with all his intense industry, and immense knowledge, he always spoke poorly of his
own powers.  " Through every part of my career,"
he says, " I have felt humbled and pulled back by
my own ignorance."  And that man was Sir Walter
Scott.  One more instance.  It is a general in his
tent who has already ridden thirty leagues to in-
spect his troops, writing a letter to one general
as to the shirts, great coats, clothes, &c., of the
regiments ; a second despatch, pressing another
general for a double stock of corn ; a third, de-
manding biscuits and bread for his troops ; a fourth,
desiring that sabres should be sent at once, and
also a supply of helmets.  He is, along with these
minute details, giving directions for the introduc-
ing of a new scheme of education, the opening of
a canal, and instructions on architecture.  Nothing,
however petty, however important, is for one moment forgotten by that general.  And his name
was among the greatest of men—Napoleon Buonaparte.

See then for yourselves from such examples how foolish and wrong it is to look down on work as unnecessary to high success. And first, then, consider the grandeur of work. Sings the poet :

"Lives of great men all remind us
    We can make our lives sublime ;
And departing leave behind us
    Footprints in the sands of time.

"Let us then be up and doing
    With a heart for any fate,
Still achieving, still pursuing,
    Learn to labour and to wait."

You are young now, and the prayer, "Give us this day our daily bread," vexes you not. You have no thought for the day, nor yet for the morrow, as to how you should live. Thank GOD for it.

But, boys, I would not bid you thank GOD for it, if the accident of birth made you look down on the poor, and those who work for life. The most vulgar of all minds is that which forgets the advice of the Epistle, "Be courteous," and thinks meanly of the poor, because he *is* poor, or yet of work as degrading.

Remember this, boys, the true nobleman, the true gentleman, may be the beggar, or the king on his throne. This first, and then remember that all work is grand and glorious, that any drudgery is divine. The maid who sweeps the room, the la-

bourer who works from morn till night in the
fields, the pettiest tradesman or mechanic, these
all, doing their works, ennoble their work, and are
ennobled by it. There is nothing vulgar in their
lives, or their work. Only then do they become
so, when they step out of their due self-respect and
ape the manners of those higher in social rank.
And, believe me, no one is so miserable as the
man who forsooth has to "kill time," who has
nothing to do, who has exhausted pleasure, whose
mind and soul are a blank. "Go to the ant, thou
sluggard; consider her ways, and be wise," preaches
Solomon. And once more; "It is better to get
wisdom than gold; for wisdom is better than
rubies, and all the things that may be desired are
not to be compared to it."

For GOD's sake, learn then that the gospel of
work is a noble gospel. Let us laugh, ay, and
heartily too. Let us thank GOD for, and praise
Him in all His gifts. Let us enjoy our life, and
the abundance of happiness smiling on every side.
But I beseech you, never regard pleasure, falsely
so called, as the one aim of life. Do good honest
work in your generation, and leave the issue to
GOD.

And secondly, and lastly, is there not much
comfort in work? When the soul is sore smitten,
and lies bruised and wounded beneath the load of
a heavy burden, well-nigh too heavy to bear—
when nothing in life seems worth having and the

soul is wrapt up in its loss, at such times activity
is a great unspeakable relief. Grasp the pain
boldly; bring yourself to face the phantom of the
past; confront your loss. Act, not only think.
Your heart will be long sore, long away from the
present life, but you will gain composure, a clear
vision of what is, and what is not, and ability to
see a gleam of sunshine in the very far horizon.
Feeling without action is, if not barren, productive
of ill Action without feeling is harsh, if not unkind. Combine the two, and sympathy will go hand
in hand with work. And in your own life, do you
not feel an inward satisfaction and a quiet gladness
after good work, genuine work, work well done ?

Well, perhaps, after all, at the end of this sermon,
you think, "this is scarcely more than an essay, an
encouragement to work, a talk about work." I
say in answer, JESUS CHRIST's whole life was one
of work. Should you not set that life before you
as a star by whose light you may walk here until
you come to "where the young Child is," even in
Heaven above?

But I would wish to see you one and all grow
up *Christian gentlemen.* I do not mean, of neces-
sity, wearing good broad cloth, nor driving in car-
riages, no, nor rich or prosperous, nor high in the
world's opinion,—all this may or may not be good
for you,—but be what the old Greeks called καλός,
"beautiful in spirit." I hope I may quote the
"Times" newspaper on this point. "That which

raises a country, that which strengthens a country, and that which dignifies a country, the true crown, throne, and sceptre of a nation; this aristocracy is not an aristocracy of blood, not one of fashion, not of talent only—it is an aristocracy of *character*. This is the true heraldry of man." Noble words are these, may you ever remember them! Preserve the grand character of a gentleman wherever you are, and never destroy your self-respect by falling below yourself. That boy well answered, who being asked why he did not steal some fruit, as nobody was there to see, said, " Yes there was, I was there to see myself."

Be and act always as Christian gentlemen, the servants of CHRIST, the sons of GOD, the brothers of all around you. Never think any work, however small and trifling, below you or not to be done with all your heart and soul. Do, instead of talking; work through difficulties and disagreeable tasks, so when at last the "night cometh when no man can work," when the great Master calls your name, you will say, *Adsum*, Here I am, and will hear these comfortable and gracious words, " Well done, good and faithful servant; enter thou into the joy of thy LORD."

## V.

## ETERNITY.

*"And I saw the dead small and great stand before God; and the books were opened: and another book was opened, which is the book of life; and the dead were judged out of those things which were written in the books according to their works."*—Rev. xx. 12.

WE must all die. Man goeth to his long home, and the mourners go about the streets. Man that is born of woman is of few days, and full of trouble. This is the LORD's doing, and man cannot gainsay it, and thousands of years have not altered the old, old story.

"Κατθανεῖν ὀφείλεται," says the Greek poet; "Omnia debemur morti," says the Roman bard; says Confucius, "The great mountain must crumble, the strong beam must break; the wise man must wither away like a plant." Ever since the day that GOD created man in His own image, and placed him all holy and immortal in the Garden of Eden, men and women and children have died,— they have died on battlefields, on the lonely heights of Alma, on the quiet field of Waterloo, where the waving corn ripens over the bones of warriors; beneath the waters of the sea. Some have died violent deaths, and in their last sad hour flung themselves into the dark waters; some have

died in their beds, and been borne in sorrow to
their last quiet home beneath waving trees, with
the music of birds, in GOD'S acre; and some sleep
in JESUS far far away in distant lands where the
stranger knows them not.

Yes, from the creation of man till now, till the
last dread trump shall wake the sleeping spirits of
the dead, man "cometh up and is cut down," yea,
he dieth, and his place knows him no more.

In speaking to you to-night, I wish very briefly
to touch on the four tremendous subjects of Death,
Judgment, Heaven, and Hell: subjects which
now I dare say seem to you very far off, for you
are in the spring-time of life. The sky of life is
clear and bright above you now, but how near
eternity may be to each one of you is in GOD'S
hands.

First then, as to Death,—it is a universal lot.
Had Adam not eaten of the fruit, man might have
lived for ever, but the sentence of death followed
his disobedience. Since that time men have been
born, sojourned here for a few years, and gone
hence. Whence they came, and whither they are
going, who can say exactly? All Nature warns us
of death,—the trees, the shrubs, the flowers, the
animal life, in all these we see change and decay.
Yes, death is universal. Yet I doubt if, as some
profess, we derive much inward satisfaction, much
quiet at heart, from this fact. True, men and
women die around us; true, not a minute passes,

but some soul is passing to its rest ; true, we only
suffer what must be, and has ever been; but does
that very much lessen our own load, our particular
heartache, our hourly daily sigh ? If it does, so
much the better; but . . . . . We see then
that no man doubts the certainty of death, but as
to what comes after death there is much difference
of thought. The Greeks and Romans in early
time thought that the souls of the departed were
escorted along by the god Mercury. In the mouth
of the dead man was placed a piece of money to
pay his passage across the ferry whereby he would
cross the river in the world below, and enter the
fields of the blessed. Two of the greatest poets of
ancient times, Homer and Virgil, have made their
chief hero pass through this world of spirits where
are the noble and brave chiefs in happiness, and
where the impious and wicked of life suffer dreadful
and unspeakable torment. The savage believed
that he would go to the hunting grounds of his
father, and be for ever happy in his favourite pas-
time of the chase. The great philosopher of China,
Confucius, can give no answer to the question,
"What of man after death ?" "While you do not
know life," he said, "what can you know about
death ?" Greek philosophy, restless and busy,
sought to solve the riddle ;—said one, "We go
into animals after this life, and our spirits live on
in the brutes around us ;" said another, "We no
sooner die, than we are born again," and thus the

life of man is ever repeating itself; said the philo-
pher Epicurus, or rather his followers, "Let us eat
and drink, for to-morrow we die;" and what says
the Bible? "After Death, the Judgment."

Boys, the world is growing old and grey. Even
as we read the history of our own land, and gaze
down the long avenues of time to the years of
England's infancy, as we read the history of the
Bible, or of the world, and trace the growth of
society, of learning, of knowledge and religion, as
we muse in thought on the "good old order" of
the thousands of years, we seem to see a little way
into eternity, we can faintly imagine what the
world will be like when the years have rolled away.
Come and stand by me in yonder quiet churchyard, where the fathers and mothers of the village
have lain side by side in peace beneath the sod so
many years ; there lie "the rude forefathers of the
hamlet,"—will you tell me they are nought but
dust? will you say that they lived their quiet
peaceful lives, went Sunday by Sunday from their
baptism to their burial to yonder ivy-clad church
for nought? Oh no! Their souls are in the hand
of GOD, and no harm can befall them. Or come
and stand by me yet again in yonder Abbey of
Westminster,—there lie the great ones of the earth,
men whose works do indeed live after them, men
whose names are household words on our lips.
Hath GOD made them for nought? Were the
fiery eloquence of Pitt, the music of Handel, the

courage of Wolfe, the silvery pen of Spenser, mere ripples in the wave of life, just a splash in the tarn whose lives have left a circle more or less broad, then have vanished altogether? Here too, believe me, no less than in the humbler sanctuary of the village house of GOD, will the Spirit of GOD move upon the face of the dead, and the soul will return to GOD Who gave it.

What a reunion will that day bring! First and foremost shall we spring to meet our loved ones, "not lost, but gone before." Into that too sacred happiness let us not too rudely look. Oh, then will they say to us, "We have long tarried for you; we have watched over you; we have been with you in your going out, and your coming in; we knelt beside you at your bedside, and our prayers mingled with yours in ascent to the throne of GOD; when you sang, your voices breathed music into our ears. We have been ever by your side, and waited for this time of perfect bliss, the dearer, the intenser, the more clinging, because of the long hours of weary waiting and absence." We will not blame Death because

"He puts our lives so far apart,
    We cannot hear each other speak."

Nay, but we can do this in spirit, and in that instinct of silent sympathy which speaks in spiritual language, gently, feelingly, and not once.

This first,—and then I take it, what an assembly

will be there! All that have ever lived from the days of Adam till the last day will be gathered round the great white throne. "And I saw the dead, both great and small, stand before GOD." We cannot grasp the thought. Imagine millions of millions of human beings, of every race and tongue, and we cannot think of one fraction of the ocean of faces that will look up into GOD's face, as the Great Judge opens the books, wherein your sins and mine, yours of forgetfulness, mine of duty, our little outburst of temper yesterday, our harsh speech of a year ago, our little error from truth, our every word of impatience, anger, impurity, unkindness, our every deed, ay, our every thought is most minutely written.

> "There is no shuffling, there the action lies
> In his true nature; and we ourselves compelled,   .
> Even to the teeth and forehead of our faults,
> To give in evidence."

Thoughts, words, deeds, long forgotten by us will rise up in action for or against us. A flash of light will kindle afresh the memory of our lives. The world praised that action,—how noble! what an act of self-sacrifice! Yet here GOD reverses the world's judgment, and condemns the motive. What a mean paltry deed! said the world; what a foolish man! GOD exalts such a one to His own right hand, and confounds the world's maxims, for He seeth not as man seeth, He seeth the heart. Can we then paint for ourselves that scene? There, at the last trump, are the quick, those then alive,—some prepared to meet their GOD, some crying to the rocks to hide them, some starting from their graves, some issuing forth from the womb of the great deep, some yielded up by the sea. For we read, "The sea gave up the dead which were in it, and death and hell delivered up the dead that were in them." "Man for judgment must prepare him."

There are Adam, Abraham, Isaac, David; there are the Apostles; there are poets, painters, authors, statesmen, generals, kings and queens, gathered from every clime, and of every tongue,—all, poor and rich, alike equal. For all have one common property, a *soul* to be saved or lost. O unspeakable anguish, if at that dread hour those whom we have dearly loved on earth stand not with us, if when the books are opened the sentence is not alike for us,—but one fond look, and never to meet again. Shall not this thought at least urge us so to live that in death we may not be divided, for can we so lose ourselves in GOD as to be absorbed in His eternal presence away from those we loved, and conscious that for them there is an eternity of misery?

But yet there remains the final doom. After Judgment comes the final sentence. Eternity of bliss, or eternity of woe! How small seems this life side by side with those words. How of passing worth the things all-important to us now, our lives, our business, our pleasures, ay, our clothes and our amusements. Is the pleasure of sixty, seventy, or eighty years to be set against the intensity of happiness or woe of "*For Ever ?*" What think you? *Eternity ! Eternity ! Eternity !* How much turns on that word ; and yet how we know nothing of its meaning. GOD has made us poor erring creatures, prone to fall and to go astray, in a world of strange contrast of pleasure and pain, of holiness and sin, of luxury and misery. He lets temptation ever cross our path, He has allowed the desire for wrong to be far stronger than that for right.

We walk only by faith in future reward, or future punishment. We see wickedness to flourish like a green bay tree, and virtue be smitten down and perish. We see many things hard to be understood. We only learn of GOD, of Judgment, of Heaven, of Hell, from one book, and only from the New Testament. We can but believe that this Book is GOD's Word to us. Yes, in this Book lie all our hopes and fears, or if not, what future can we have?

I say then, can it be that such a life of but a few short hours, or rather seconds, compared to eternity, shall be rewarded or punished by an ever-ending sentence? Is this in accordance with GOD's dealings to us in this life? Can it be that GOD will condemn man beyond hope of recovery,—give

him no chance of turning from perpetual misery?
I cannot, I dare not say. We look around us in
this life, the world changes not, the trees and
flowers delight us still, winter, spring, summer and
autumn come and go, all things continue as they
were from the beginning. We cannot realise these
vast mysteries, only at a few moments when we
stand in the awful presence of death, when we go
just a step with the dead out of this world, does
the dread reality seize our whole spirits.

I have no time to-night to speak to you of that
future state; and if I had, what more could I
tell than what we all learn from the Bible itself?
As for that kingdom of GOD, that better land,
eye hath not seen, nor ear heard, nor hath it
entered into the heart of man to conceive, the joys
to be found at GOD's right hand. In our FA-
THER's presence will all tears be wiped away, the
partings of this life shall be lost in eternal presence, our whole bodies and souls will be purified
and made meet for that city. There is no sanctuary of GOD, for GOD's presence is itself an everlasting shrine of holiness; there prayer is lost in
praise. Whether we may there follow out to perfection our favourite pursuits on earth; whether
those who have died in childhood will always be
children there; whether we shall at once, or step
by step, rise to supreme happiness, we know not,
though we may often think on such things.

And as it should at all times be a dear thought

to us to think of that world beyond the sky, so unspeakably sad is the abode of the wicked. For however distasteful and bitter to us, still we cannot away with the word of GOD Himself,—"The wicked shall be turned into hell, and all the people that forget GOD." O if you would go to the bright heavenly land, if you would escape the sorrow and anguish of the second death, if you would join the communion of saints, think on these things. Put your thoughts into practice. Turn to GOD now while you are young, and are not tied and bound by the chain of your sins. Then, so living, will you fall asleep in JESUS, and through the grave and gate of death pass to your joyful resurrection, and be

"For ever with the LORD."

"Safe home, safe home in port,
　　Rent cordage, shattered deck ;
　Torn sails, provisions short,
　　And only not a wreck ;
　But oh the joy upon the shore
　To tell our voyage perils o'er.

"The exile is at home,
　　O nights and days of tears,
　O longings not to roam,
　　O sins, and doubts, and fears !
　What matters now grief's darkest day,
　When GOD has wiped all tears away?"

## VI.

## GODLY, NOT GODLESS.

*" Without God."*—Eph. ii. 12.

Boys, picture to yourselves the seaside—when the rays of the sun are dancing on the blue sea, and land and sea alike are shining in the warmth and light of a summer's day.   There is a large bay, and within this bay there are ships and fishing boats at anchor : the water within the bay is calm, and the tiny waves roll upon the sand which glistens with many coloured shells.   There are three boys strolling along the beach, picking up shells ; but as the afternoon goes on, the eldest of them gets tired of this, and proposes to the other two that they should unloose a boat which is lying high and dry upon the beach and put out to sea in it.   The second boy would like to go very much, but his father has forbidden him.   " It is very hard," he says, " it's such a splendid day for a row, and the water looks so tempting."   And the youngest one, what does he say and do ?   " No," he says, it is not right to go, that their father no doubt had some wise reason for forbidding their going in a boat on the sea.   But the eldest insists on going.   He will go alone if the other two won't go.   He laughs at the idea of danger; how can there be danger when the sea is so still, and all looks bright and beau-

tiful? And first the second boy little by little gives
way; and at last the youngest agrees, and they
push off from land. That youngest brother feels
half-inclined even now to jump out and return
home: perhaps in his mind he hears his mother's
voice reading a verse out of the Book of Samuel,
"To obey is better than sacrifice;" and he thinks
of the lessons he has learnt at her knee, when she
taught him Sunday stories out of the big Bible,
and he recalls his father's face and look of approval
when he did something right. But he hesitates;
they row out further, and further, and further.
And now it is too late to jump out, and swim back
to land. All goes well for some time, and they
are now just outside the bay. They will row past
some high rocks under the cliffs, and get out and
bathe again. But meantime they have not no-
ticed that dark, sullen clouds have come up over-
head faster and faster; and now the sea becomes
rougher and more angry each minute. They turn,
and try to row back, but there are now breakers
lashing themselves upon the shore, and the great
white sea-horses of foam are rushing along one
after another, threatening to swallow up the little
boat. Suddenly, one boy loses hold of his oar:
in trying to pick it up, the other is lost. And now
they are in the midst of the sea, outside the bay,
with none to help, and danger on every side,—and
there let us leave them.

Boys, would you wish to be like them? Would

you be far out at sea, without an anchor, without
a pilot, with no one to aid you—and alone? Yet,
believe me, this is no mere picture, but it is the
fact. Those who love you, and strive for your
good, would grieve beyond everything that you
should be thus helpless. You are too young to be
so now, but if you are wise you will take warning
now, and believe the teaching of those who are
wiser and older than you.

And what does this story mean, that I have
been setting before you to-night? I will tell you.
These boys on the open sea, helpless and doomed
to perish, are an emblem, a likeness, a picture of
all those who are living without GOD in the world.
Such are not only without GOD, living away from
Him, regardless of Him, but they are also in the
midst of the waves of this cold, selfish, and hard
world. And such may you and I be, if we do
not fix our anchor safe in CHRIST and His great
mercy. You know the expression, a "man of the
world"—do you know exactly what it means?
Well, it means the opposite of a man of GOD.
You read in the Bible of Enoch who walked with
GOD, and of David, "the man after GOD's own
heart," and in the New Testament of S. John, the
disciple whom JESUS loved. All these were men
of GOD. They no doubt fell back at times, and
went wrong ; they were not perfect, they were men
of like weakness and passions with ourselves ; but
they sought after what was good and noble, and

true and pure, and when they went wrong they turned to GOD, and begged for His forgiveness to blot out their sins.

Let me to-night very shortly sketch out for you two such opposite lives as those of the " man of GOD" and the " man of the world," and choose for yourselves which is the better to follow. And first, let me tell you that the old Greeks even knew well that it is in youth that the choice between these two is made. For once upon a time there was a great hero and a god named Hercules, the strongest man of old Greek history, and very much like Samson of the Bible. And when he was quite young he sat down where two roads met, and wondered which to take, and as he thus sat hesitating, two women came up to him, one dressed out gaudily and with a bold manner, the other simply dressed, and quiet. And the first one begged him to walk along her road, which was strewn with flowers and easy for walking; on *her* road, she said, were no rugged places, no hills to climb, but all was pleasant and easy—and her name was Vice. But the other said, " O Hercules, walk in my road : it is indeed difficult and rugged, and there are stones and rocks in the way, and ofttimes you will be weary and footsore. Yet there are not, as on the other road, pitfalls concealed by flowers and dark holes into which you will fall unawares. And the road whereby I will lead you will bring you to the fields of the blessed, where there is sunny joy and happiness for ever." And I am glad to say, boys, that Hercules made a wise choice, and followed this second speaker, whose name was Virtue.

First, then, there is the boy who perhaps from infancy is badly brought up, and as soon as he is born goes astray and does wrong; or it may be, he has been well and carefully taught, has had a loving mother and a father's care watching over him to shield him from evil. He goes to school with many a tender prayer, and GOD-speed from mother and father. And for awhile he goes on well, and makes good resolutions. But he depends on himself, he thinks he can stand by himself and do right without GOD's help : and he forgets the solemn warning of a wise Apostle, "Let him that thinketh he standeth take heed lest he fall." He says his prayers hurriedly; if he is late in the morning he shortens them, and at times leaves them altogether unsaid. He finds it so much easier to do what is wrong, and it seems such uphill work, such a struggle, to be always trying to do what is right. And now that he does not pray, or only prays with his lips, but his heart remains behind, he has no pilot to guide his boat; he has no hand to help him. O GOD, help him now, for he has thrown aside the GOD of his youth : he has forgotten to look to his FATHER in heaven; he looks back at times to the time when he first lisped out his childish prayers; he would do right, he would like to be good, but he will not

make the effort, and in the terrible words of the
Bible, "GOD is gone from him."

My dear boys, I pray GOD this may never be
your case. Yet, believe me, this may be so ; for
we do not become bad all at once ; it is by little
daily acts, by little sins, by little untruths, now and
then yielding to temper, or sloth, or selfishness, or
the like, that step by step, inch by inch, our character becomes worse and worse. We are not
worse at once ; the course of evil begins so slowly,
and from such slight source. "An infant's hand
might stop the breach with clay." We drift away
into sin, we do not boldly strike out for it, but we
lay down our oars, and are carried out by the tide
far from the shore of our childhood's purity and
goodness. Ah, well it is for such a one if after
a wasted life and years of pleasure, falsely so
called, he arise and say, "I will go unto My FA-
THER."

But, thank GOD, there is the other side of the
picture. There is the boy who comes to school,
determined to remember the lessons of home and
the voice of his conscience. He knows that
he is much happier, much brighter, much better
every way for doing GOD's will, and acting rightly.
He falls at times ; perhaps at a sudden moment
taken off his guard he tells a lie ; at times he feels
lazy, and disinclined to apply himself to work ; at
times he thinks only of himself, and his own pleasure,
and thinks little that he is cowardly, and paining

some one younger and weaker than himself. Now and again his temper gets the better of him, and he thinks this rule hard, and that punishment severe. Yet through all these slips—yes, and falls too—he struggles on, doing his duty to GOD, and his duty to man too. Oh, believe me, such a life is most blessed. For such a one is serving GOD in the golden time of boyhood, in the springtime of life, and passes from his young days to manhood and its new temptations and trials, strong in the strength which GOD supplies, and with a character formed for good by past experience. Which of these two would you be like? The one brings may be sorrow to his home, disgrace on himself. If not this, he goes through life making none happier and better by kindness and unselfishness, and having lived without GOD in the world, he dies, uncared for, unloved, unready to meet his GOD. But the memory of the just is blessed. And he who from boyhood has honestly tried to walk with GOD and to do his little good in this life will hear the comforting words, " Well done, thou good and faithful servant, enter thou into the joy of thy LORD."

Do you now, while it is called To-day, while you are easily moved to right, while evil has not taken deep root in your hearts, believe in and cling to Him, Who alone can give you that peace which the world cannot give. And so will you from your hearts be able to exclaim with a good hope,—

"O GOD, my help in ages past,
    My hope for years to come,
    My shelter from the stormy blast,
    And my eternal home."

To which may GOD bring us all, for CHRIST'S
sake.

---

## VII.

## SYMPATHY.

*"Am I my brother's keeper?"*—Gen. iv. 9.

I HAVE been reading this week past of a great
man who died a little while ago. His name was
Selwyn, and he was Bishop of Lichfield. And I
wish you this evening just for a very few minutes
to think of his life, and to see for yourselves how
this servant of GOD brought others to CHRIST, and
was a true faithful keeper of the souls under his
charge.

Bishop Selwyn was at Eton as his school, and
always remembered it with the deepest love. He
was appointed to be Bishop of New Zealand, and
obeyed the call at once, and went out into that
far-off land to labour for CHRIST, and to bring
mankind into His fold. Bishop Selwyn was well
fitted for the post, both in body and spirit. He
was able to swim a river, to ride an unmanageable

horse, to handle a ship with such skill that an old
sailor declared " that to see it was enough to make
a man a Christian," and at the same time he set
before himself as his one high object in life to save
the souls of the poor heathen who were in darkness
groping after light and after GOD, if haply they
might find Him.

For a great number of years he worked on, living a hard life of self-denial, and winning many
souls from darkness to light. The time came at
length when the Bishopric of Lichfield was offered
him; and he took it with many a pang at leaving
the scene of his labours, and the people whom he
loved so well. How they loved him is best set
forth in the touching and simple words of the poor
islanders.

"To Bishop Selwyn greeting. Go to your own
country; go on the face of the deep waters.
Father, take hence the commandments of GOD,
leaving the people here bewildered. Our love for
you, and our remembrance of you will never cease.
Enough. This concludes our words of farewell to
you. From your children."

He lived again here in England a like life of
self-sacrifice and stern hard work; and at length
after more than fifty years of bringing brethren to
CHRIST he has passed away, doubtless to meet
again many who have reached Heaven under his
guidance and brotherly care. And I ask you, Is
this not a noble life, a life that makes the world

nobler and better, for such a man having lived in
it, a life that was a ladder set up on earth, upon
which poor fainting souls of men ascended to
Heaven?

And if we turn from such a life to think on the
words of Cain, "Am I my brother's keeper?" can
we doubt what the answer is? No, we cannot.
Yet do we often live as though we with Cain asked
this question.

And if I have pointed you to such a life as Bishop
Selwyn's, how can I not point you to the perfect
picture of that most noble missionary whose sacred
feet trod this poor earth of ours, the Man JESUS
CHRIST? None so poor, none so feeble, none so
vile, but He would bring them to Himself. His ·
everlasting arms were ever open to receive the
doubting Thomas, the sinning Magdalene, the denying Peter, the thief on the cross. "Come unto
Me, all that are weary and heavy laden, and I
will give you rest." Oh, words laden with comfort
to the burdened soul! Oh, welcome that says to
none, "Too late—you cannot enter now." Are
not the words of my text, "Am I my brother's
keeper?" answered indeed by such a life as this?
"He went about doing good," says the Evangelist.
Wherever He went, virtue went out of Him.
Whatever He said, was a message to mankind;
whatever He did, was a mission of love to a lost
world. And to such a noble example have thousands of saints of GOD looked, since He, the light

to lighten the Gentiles, was taken away from us. An imitation of such a life does the missionary live, who toils far away from his home and kindred, in ofttimes desert or fevered lands, with none to aid him or soothe him in his weariness. Such a life does many a clergyman live in the slums and alleys of our great cities, bringing the poor, the maimed, the halt and the blind to CHRIST, if only they may touch the hem of His garment.

Such a life leads the Sister of Mercy in our great hospitals and streets, braving sickness and death, counting all danger as nothing, so only she may win souls to GOD. And such a life do all those live, rich or poor, strong or weak, old or young, who are doing angel's work below, and sowing the good seed of eternal life.

And how may you in your life here and at home, both now and in after time, act as your brother's keeper? Is it not enough for us, perhaps, you think, if we can do right ourselves and obey GOD's commandments? Yet, I will try to show you two ways in which it seems to me you may thus bring your brethren to CHRIST, young though you are, and small though the field be in which as yet you work. And then we will conclude by looking at the unspeakable blessing which will follow from such a course of action.

First, then, we can do much good to others by example, by silent example. A life preaches. No text is so eloquent as a life that is an imitation of

CHRIST. And the example of a holy life in our midst, though it put forward no pretensions, and make no great outward show, possesses a wide influence for good, which cannot but be felt; and example seems to divide itself into passive and active example.

Passive example I would call that of a life that we read of or hear of,—such a life as I have been speaking of to you to-night. A book, a hymn, poetry, music, a beautiful view, or the like, may exercise a very good influence over us. They may recall to us something that we have once loved and have lost: they may make us once more to wander in the happy fields of clear and blessed memories: they may stir up in us a fresh impulse for good. You go into a cathedral, and you hear the sacred music pealing through the nave and aisles; the sweet music seems to thrill you through and through, and you are taken for a little while out of the outside clatter and heat and din of the world, and caught up into a little sweetness, a brief foretaste of perfect repose.

These examples are all passive. They cannot of themselves take us by the hand and lead us upwards. They are but strong enough to point us to the road that we must travel, they are but signposts directing us how to walk. More they cannot be. Example must be also *active*. And here again I will refer you to the life of one whom some of you at least have heard of, who was head master

of a large school near here. I refer to Dr. Arnold. He was his brother's keeper, if ever man
was. He entered Rugby school at a time when
influence for good was little known ; and little by
little, like leaven, his good influence spread throughout the whole school. Sunday after Sunday he
stood up in that school chapel and pleaded for his
Master, in accents that urged goodness and re-
buked vice. Week after week he held up before
their sight a noble example of truthfulness, purity,
and manliness. A seeker after GOD himself, he
led his boys to seek after GOD. Such a life being
dead yet speaketh.

And I would ask you to think to-night how
awful is this power of influence, which we one and
all have. Some have it far more than others.
Some are put into positions of trust and dignity,
where they must lead those below them. All of
us should reflect that we are responsible to others
as well as to ourselves for our words and deeds.
You, one and all, may influence those about you.
You do so influence them day by day. If one boy
is more clever, more strong, more popular than
others, he is likely to be looked up to. His actions may be set up as a standard for the others to
follow. Such a boy has a great responsibility.
GOD has given him more talents than others, and
he may not hide them in a napkin : they are not
his, but GOD's. But with the increase of talents,
comes an increase of responsibility. You see this

all round you : you hear a great preacher, swaying
his audience by his eloquence : you read the book
of a great author, who leads you along with his
words like a little child : you see a great painter's
work, which suggests to you thoughts unfelt before.
Such men are leaders of life : but let them beware
lest they offend, or put a stumbling-block in the
way of those who follow. For as to you, boys, it
is a blessed thing to set up a high standard of
goodness to which the younger and weaker may
look for guidance : so it is a cursed thing, if you
set a bad example, and lead those who follow you
into the paths of sin. If you misuse your talents,
your greater age, your greater knowledge, your
more strength, your talents will be no blessing to
you, but a curse.

And this brings me to the second way in which
you may lead others to CHRIST : and that is, you
must do more than set an example which may
guide others, you must advise to good, you must
utter a word of warning to those about to sin, you
must speak a word of encouragement to those who
are doubtful and fearful, lest they fall. Do you
say to me, We are too young to be thus missionaries for GOD, we cannot do more than save
ourselves from wrong? I answer, Samuel was not
too young to speak the word of GOD to the aged
priest Eli; you are not too young to die; so you
are not too young to live rightly yourselves, and
quietly to teach others so to live. If temptation

comes, and one of you hesitates, think perhaps not
only you yourself will fall, but you will drag others
with you. Rather remember that those weaker
than you may be wishing to resist the temptation,
and would do so of themselves ; but they look to
you, to see what you will do. You are, then, their
keeper.

And, lastly, remember the unspeakable blessing
that follows such a life, and how awful is a life
which has kept others away from GOD. No more
awful words are in the Bible than these ; " Whoso
shall offend one of these little ones that believe in
Me, it were better for him that a mill-stone were
hanged about his neck, and that he were drowned
in the depth of the sea." Can there be a sadder
picture than to look back not merely on a wasted
life, a life without GOD, but more, on a life that
has put hindrances in the way of those who else
had lived lives of holiness ? And as this memory
is of all memories the most dreadful, so unspeakably happy must be the memory of souls saved by
may be a few words spoken in season, by good
advice, by the example of an upright and pure
heart. Will it not be indeed a cause to such an
one of the deepest joy to meet in the world beyond
those who have gained paradise under GOD by his
guidance ? How blessed to have turned but one
sinner from the error of his ways, and to have set
him on the rock which is ever safe ! Think of
such a prospect, and try from boyhood upwards to

set yourselves to show forth a good light that may shine in a naughty world, and to lead gently those who are younger, feebler, more exposed to temptation—not rudely, not carelessly, but regarding them as most precious, and very dear to the great Shepherd CHRIST JESUS, Who has told us "that in Heaven their angels do always behold the face of My FATHER Which is in Heaven."

> " To comfort and to bless,
>    To find a balm for woe,
> To tend the lone and fatherless,
>    Is angel's work below.
> The captive to release,
>    To GOD the lost to bring,
> To teach the way of life and peace,
>    It is a CHRIST-like thing."

---

## VIII.

## THE TRINITY.

*" How can these things be ?"*—S. John iii. 9.

I WAS a child, and I opened my eyes to find myself in the midst of a vast plain; on all sides of me there was nothing but one flat surface, bounded by no hills, and with no valleys to break the dull monotony of the scene; and I knew not how I had come to be here, although now and again

flashes of memory came across me at very rare
intervals, as though I had seen this flower on that
field, or part of the scene before—and there were
many other children in this wide plain, some play-
ing heedlessly, some picking flowers, and some,
only a few, walking steadily on towards the distant
horizon, and I wondered at them, and asked them
who had set them down in this plain.   But they
said, "We know nothing, we are like you, set upon
this plain, not of ourselves, and we are bidden to
move forwards towards the distant horizon, for we
are told, and we believe, there is a land there, where
there is a great pleasure ground, and where all is
not a dull plain as this is, and we desire to see this
better country."   And I heard many of the children
laugh at these words and say, "Who has told you
this?   Who believes these stories?   No one has
ever come back to tell us that the flowers there are
far brighter than the flowers here; or, that the sky
there is a deeper blue and far more lovely than this
sky."   And when these children thus laughed, I
thought that after all, this anxiety to get on, this
exertion of walking day after day, might be all in
vain.   For indeed it did seem much more pleasant
to pick the flowers, and to eat the ripe and beautiful
fruit which was growing all round; and then the
children did not after all know for certain whence
they came, or whither they were going.   So I said
to one who was keeping his eyes steadily upon the
horizon in front, "But who has advised you thus

F

to walk? And have you any guide who has ever shown you the way?" And he said, "Child, that is indeed our FATHER Who lives in this far off land, and is very good and great, and calls us all His children; none of us have ever seen Him, but we have heard much of Him, though He has never been to this plain Himself: and perhaps therefore we should have missed the way, only we have also an elder Brother who came here to help us, and point out to us the way, and took all the trouble to walk in it Himself." And I asked, "Did He leave that happy land you speak of to come here just for your sake and mine?" "Yes," said the boy, "and He was laughed at by all the children then here, far more than we are, and they did all they could to hurt Him, but He never took His eyes off the horizon behind which is this land of promise." But I said, "That is long ago, is it not? and how can you be sure, now that you have lost Him, that you are always walking in the right direction? for there are many, very many paths on this land." And he answered, "O yes, but we have also an elder Sister who is so loving and gentle, and who whispers at times to us which is the right path; and we do all at times miss our road, (only our elder Brother ever went *quite* straight,) and we sometimes fall into pits which are hidden here and there: but our elder Sister never quite leaves us, and her voice is so sad and sweet, that we are all ashamed to displease her." And then I awoke, and behold it was all a dream.

" So runs my dream, but what am I ?
   An infant crying for the night ;
   An infant crying for the light,
   And with no language but a cry."

My dear boys, I wish to say a few words to you to-night on the lessons of to-day, which is called Trinity Sunday; and perhaps this allegory may help you a little to understand it. It, " The Trinity," is a great mystery, one of many mysteries which we cannot understand in this life. We, like those children, must walk by Faith. There are very many things hidden from our sight by GOD.

" Whence we came, and whither wending,"

we know not, what GOD is, what Heaven and hell are, what is the fate of those gone before, what is our fate, we know not. Our life is as the plain on which those children walked, and one and all

" We are such stuff as dreams are made of."

And the doctrine of the Trinity, Three Persons, the FATHER, the SON, and the HOLY GHOST in One, is a very great mystery, and makes us ask with Nicodemus, " How can these things be ?" And having asked this question, are we not·where we were before ? Since the days of Adam, wise men of all nations have tried to read the writing, and expound the riddle of life, but none have been found in whom the Spirit of GOD is to read it aright for the satisfaction of all. Let us then leave this and other mysteries in GOD's hands,—and where can we better leave them?—and for a few minutes to-night ask ourselves, one and all, what has this Godhead with its three Persons, GOD the FATHER, GOD the SON, and GOD the HOLY GHOST, done for me, yes, and is doing daily for me? In my allegory, or little story, I told you of the great FATHER, the elder Brother, the elder Sister. May I, with all reverence speak of the three Persons of the Trinity as such?

Firstly. Is not GOD our FATHER? Do we not pray to Him as "Our FATHER Which art in Heaven?"

Every nation from its very earliest times has felt that there must be a something or somebody far higher, and nobler, and greater than man; a somebody who could create and destroy. The savage worshipped stocks, and stones, and idols. The Greek called upon Father Zeus who lived in a mountain called Olympus, the top of which was ever hid from man's eye by a sacred mist. The Roman cried to Jupiter as the greatest God in Heaven. These men saw GOD in all His works, they thought that He was in the rivers, the caves, the springs, the trees, and ignorant as they were of the true GOD, yet they believed Him to be everywhere. There has always been a feeling more or less strong in all mankind, that this world, and all that is in it, is not the work of chance, not the work of rude and hasty workmanship, but the perfect product of some Power infinite, all-powerful and eternal. This Power *we know is God.* "In the beginning," we read, "GOD made the heavens and

the earth." There have been men who have tried
to prove other causes for the creation and preser-
vation of this world. You perhaps know the story
of the Emperor Napoleon Buonaparte, who, after
listening to some wise men trying to prove that not
GOD, but other causes created this world, pointed
with his hand to the stars in their courses shining
on their heavenly way in the firmament above, and
said, "Yes, gentlemen, but who made all those?"
Such men have always failed, and after denying
GOD in this life, have cried to Him in their death
with an exceeding bitter cry. Such was the end of
a very great and able French writer named Voltaire,
who had professed all his life with the fool in the
Psalms, that there is no GOD, and had therefore
defied GOD in all His actions, careless of a future
life, and of the righteous Judgment. Yet, on his
death, he was obliged to admit to his friends
gathered round his bed, that, "If there were no
GOD, it would be necessary to invent one !"

And GOD has not only made this world, and
put therein man, fearfully and wonderfully made :
He preserves this·world in all its beauty and wonder. He has placed on high myriads of stars that
we see in the long wintry nights shining in heaven ;
He has clothed the earth with green grass, afford-
ing food for beasts, and pleasant to the eye ; He
hath made the great and wide sea also. "All this
hath GOD done, and we perceive that it is His
work." Ought not this to make us cry aloud with

all our hearts, "O that men would therefore praise the LORD for His goodness, and declare the wonders that He doeth to the children of men !" But GOD has done more for us, He has given to you and to me much more near and dear gifts even than these. All the mighty works of GOD make us admire Him, as " He plants His footsteps on the sea, and rides upon the storm." We fear Him in the fire, the storm, the earthquake ; but we love Him as our FATHER for the gifts which He pours upon us, and for which, what return can we make Him ? In the words of that most beautiful hymn—

> "For peaceful homes and healthful days,
> For all the blessings earth displays,
> We owe Thee thankfulness and praise,
> Who givest all."

Think, each one of you boys, what would be your position if you had no loving ones at home to think of you and love you,—if no father or mother or brothers or sisters cared for you ; if you were smitten down by constant pain or ill-health, so that life became very hard to bear ; if grief and suffering were your portion here, what would life be without a thing to love? Do any of you know what it is to have lost one you have loved? or to have been laid for a long time on a bed of sickness ? I feel sure you would think this very wretched and very sad. All these blessings GOD has given you, and you have done nothing to deserve them.

And then, as it seems to me, lest GOD the FA-
THER should notwithstanding all this unspeakable
goodness and wealth of tender mercies seem too
far removed from us; lest we should say, "Thou
art in Heaven and I upon earth, I cannot grasp
or feel all this," comes to us, *secondly*, GOD the
SON, the Man CHRIST JESUS. He is GOD equal
with the FATHER, but yet He is Man, our Elder
Brother. When missionaries have gone to the
heathen, and have spoken to them of GOD the
FATHER, and of His tremendous majesty and
power, these ignorant savages have said, "O, yes,
we know about the Great Spirit, your GOD. He is
the GOD Who sweeps along upon the wings of the
rushing mighty wind through the dark pine forests;
He is the GOD Who hides His face at times, and
makes the sun dark behind a cloud; He is the
GOD Who breathes hotly on the ground, and all
thereon dies; He is the GOD Who makes the sea
stand on a heap, and lashes the waves into fury of
mountain height. · We have heard, and do know
this GOD." And the missionaries find that GOD
the FATHER does not attract them,—they fear Him
too much. But when they say to the savages,
"We also tell you of One Who left the glory that
He had with the FATHER in Heaven to live among
men; Who was in all respects like as we are, except without sin; Who was tempted, a Man of
sorrows, persecuted, hung on the shameful cross,
that all men, heathen and Christian alike, might

be brought back from sin; Who has said, 'Come unto Me, and I will give you rest;'" then the savages are strangely moved by this life of CHRIST, lived so many hundreds of years ago in a far-off part of the world.    It needs not that I tell you of that life, for it is a life which should be written in our hearts, a life of all lives the most tender and beautiful that this world can ever see or hear of.    Yes, we need no prophet, no preacher, nothing to enlarge on the love of CHRIST Who died for us when we were yet sinners.

> "There is a green hill far away,
>     Without a city wall,
>   Where the dear LORD was crucified,
>     Who died to save us all."

On that green hill far away we will leave our dear LORD; yes, and we will take our sorrows, our wants, and our prayers there, for

> "Dearly, dearly has He loved,
>   And we must love Him too."

Yes, CHRIST went away from earth.    We cannot go to Him Himself now in time of need; He is gone from our sight for a little while back to His FATHER'S throne.    He has left us One Who is perfect GOD likewise, Whose breath hovers round us all our lives, if we will only walk in the pure fresh air of GOD's commandments.

Yes, thirdly, GOD the HOLY SPIRIT is ever with us, unless we drive Him away.    As we read that the

Spirit of GOD moved upon the face of the waters in the infancy of the world's creation, so the same Spirit attends our actions, makes us every one holy, and our bodies His temple. Does the HOLY SPIRIT seem to you something vague and indefinite? Yet CHRIST says distinctly, "He shall be *with* you, and shall be *in* you." Only the world cannot receive this Spirit of truth, because the world can neither see Him nor know Him. Yet this Spirit has in days gone by made weak women and little children, in time of persecution, as well as men, endure suffering and death, for He has guided them by His right hand into all truth. They were not comfortless in their hour of need, for they had a Comforter in their souls to inspire them with inward confidence and peace. Is not this memory, that GOD'S Spirit has chosen your soul and body for His abiding place, a memory awful indeed, yet full of comfort? For in your body and soul the Comforter rears up an Altar, and you can worship thereby day by day. Your bodies are as a Church consecrated and set apart for the special use of this most HOLY GHOST. Therefore must you and I beware lest anything wrong, or impure, or foolish, or selfish, or evil enter therein. Where GOD'S Spirit is, there cannot be sin. There is a place in a great play called "Faust," where the man, who is really the evil spirit, Satan, in disguise, tries to force his way amid the crowd of maidens and men in a village scene: but they

make the sign of the cross to him, and, powerless
to hurt, he shrinks away in pain and terror.　So
look you, I beg, that you keep your souls and
bodies only for this blessed Guest.　Impurity cannot enter there, for GOD the Spirit is of purer
eyes than to behold sin; selfishness can find no
room there, for the Spirit says we must love GOD
and our neighbour, and omits all mention of loving self.　No evil can breathe in those hallowed
precincts.

Such is the work of the Trinity,—Three in One,
and One in Three.　We cannot explain or understand it.　We must rest content to say with Nicodemus, "How can these things be?"　We walk in
darkness it is true, but yet we have a star that
ever goes before us.　Let us walk in our way
through life with GOD, as remembering, "Thou
GOD seest me."　Let us hold fast to CHRIST's
hand, Who loved us, and gave Himself for us.
Let us listen to the gentle voice of that HOLY
SPIRIT Who shall guide us into all truth.　So,
though we cannot always see our path, we may say
with good courage,

> " Lead, kindly Light, amid the encircling gloom,
>   　　Lead Thou me on :
> 　The night is dark, and I am far from home,
> 　　　Lead Thou me on.
> 　Keep Thou my feet, I do not ask to see
> 　The distant scene, one step enough for me."

## IX.

## FRIENDSHIP.

*" There is a friend that sticketh closer than a brother."—*
Proverbs xviii. 24.

IT is early dawn. The sun in his new risen
strength is breaking forth into smiles over the blue
sea. By the quay in yonder port two ships are
equipping themselves to start on the long and
perilous voyage of discovery; they are sister ships,
and belong to one owner. How busy is the scene
on board! how men are hurrying to and fro to put
everything in order! how gallantly they set forth,
the white sails gleaming in the sunshine! for a
while we can watch them from the shore, and at
first the twin vessels keep nigh to one another, as
though the presence of one inspired confidence in
the other. Thus they proceed on their journey,
exchanging words of mutual cheeriness, or at least
signals expressive of good will and present pros-
perity. But night comes on; the two vessels try to
keep near each other, but the darkness and the
rising waves little by little drive them apart. The
cold grey morning breaks upon them with driving
rain and a windy tempest; they are no longer
united, but many weary miles of barren sea hold
them apart. So it is for many a long day; at rare
intervals they flash signals to each other, and right

happy are the crew when wind and weather permit this.   But at length after days of weary separation, they meet again on the other side of this great sea, and lie side by side in the haven where they would be, happy and at peace.

Such is a picture sung of by the poet of the course of the life of each of us.   We one and all start forth in the morning of our lives, with, let us hope, some one—a father, mother, brother, sister, friend—whom we dearly love.   But as the evil day comes on, separation must take place, clouds come across our sky, our dear ones must go for a while from us, the boy goes from home to school, the young man goes out into the world, the mother loses her daughter.   These partings must needs be in life; and the home which contained so many seeds of love, the home which was for a long time the scene of all our best and truest thoughts, is lost to us.   The members of the family go forth and are divided, and the memory of long winter evenings round the glowing fire, with a father reading aloud, of summer evenings when we all sat out together in the garden, and watched the shadows slowly lengthening, is a memory, nothing more.

To-night, by GOD's help, I would point out to you a few of the uses of earthly friendship in this life; how we may sanctify friendship among our friends, how, even if GOD denies us friendship, or leaves us to pass through the waters of life alone, He is our great Friend, Who sticketh closer than a brother.

The subject of friendship cannot but be one which enters largely into school life. The true ideal or standard of friendship we can admire in the beautiful story of David and Jonathan, how the son of the King of Israel loved the shepherd boy David with a love "passing the love of women." Such love 'twixt friend and friend is not a thing to scoff at, it is a holy and blessed thing, which may GOD grant to one and all of you.

First then, there seems to be something peculiarly touching in the *instinct* of friendship. GOD forbid that I should depreciate or say one word to make you think less of "the spell of home affection," but there is this difference between a true real friendship and a home affection, that on the one hand we are placed among loving hearts, not of our own choosing but by GOD's appointment; whereas on the other hand we choose out for ourselves our friends or friend (for there is only one, or a few, to whom we grudgingly can accord our dearest affection.) How this instinct grows we cannot say; why we pick out our friend out of the crowd we may not always know. We feel strangely moved by affection to some, we feel we have an instinct of affection peculiar to ourselves "and a stranger doth not intermeddle with it." Such love does by no means exclude a universal love; the one we retain in a "holy of holies," the other we possess in the outer court.

Secondly; the *use* of friendship is great, we are by

nature prone to lean on one another all our lives. The babe on opening its eyes on this world clings to its mother's bosom, it holds fast to its parents in infancy, and grows up under their wing. And so it is through life ; how many of us are weak compared to the strong ! Do we not turn instinctively and with a feeling of imitation to the superior mind and the stronger will? We have our friendships everywhere in this world; each and all is a link in the chain which binds us to GOD, and as each link breaks off, we stand nearer and nearer to the presence of GOD Himself, our FATHER in Heaven.

A great author, a great poet, a book, a letter, music, flowers, all these may be friends, they may be friends valuable alone to us, (I take it there is nothing *morbid* in this,) they set before us the workings of a great and noble mind, they appeal to our best feelings, they take us by the hand and disclose the nakedness of sin and sorrow, and surprise us in our sloth and indifference to the sadness of the poor; they recall a sacred joy and snatches of happiness living for us, only to be hugged to our breast in blest memory. Some of us feel a deep friendship for books; we have our favourites whom we bring forth in our leisure moments, and love to commune with quietly, whose passages create in us a world of unfelt thought, and exactly suit our feeling of the moment.

You, boys, can well know the blessing and value of a friend ; it is no light thing, believe me, to have

some one in whom we can entirely trust, to whom
we can speak out our real mind, and cast off all
artificiality and reserve of feeling. Such a friend,
be it man, woman, or child, loves us through all our
faults, tells us our faults, advises us in difficulties,
warns us in our times of conceit, comforts us in
our sorrows. Such an one may be taken for a while
from us, we may only hear at brief intervals of him;
with increasing years increasing difference of thought
may arise. But where there has been true genuine
friendship, it can never die. And should it please
GOD to take our friend to Himself, and to leave
us alone without his help, we feel in the bitter
wrench what we have lost, and yet in the memory
of all the days that have been, we can truly say,

> " 'Tis better to have loved and lost
> Than never to have loved at all."

Thirdly; then there seem to me to be two con-
ditions of friendship, each necessary; first, truthfulness; second, sympathy. There must be nothing
between you and your friend; of course you will
differ in opinion, your likes and dislikes will not be
the same, but you must know each other's heart.
True friendship does not always say and do what is
pleasant; while it loves, it also respects truth and
duty. It is strange how one little concealment
may mar unclouded intercourse; you keep something back, not bigger than a man's hand, and it
grows, and grows, and grows, into a great cloud.

Thence follow misunderstandings and quarrels, dislikes and heart-burns, and may be estrangement,
which alas must ever be in our life here, I suppose,
for, as the poet sings,

> "Constancy lives in realms above,
>   And life is thorny and youth is vain,
> And to be wroth with one we love
>   Doth work like madness in the brain."

Don't be afraid of telling your friend his faults,
always in the spirit of meekness, as knowing yourself to be full of faults ; he will respect you as well
as love you all the more, and you may be the
means of saving a soul to God.   We read in the old
story, that when King Arthur lay a-dying, he begged
his friend Sir Bedivere to take his well beloved
and splendid sword Excalibur, and to cast it into
the Mere.   Twice did Bedivere deceive him, and
fail in his mission, though he. meant it kindly.
Was this well? was this the part of a true friend?
No, therefore remember you, that calling good
evil, and evil good, is not the part of such a friend
as you should be.   And besides truthfulness, a
friend must have *sympathy*.   There are plenty of
people, I dare say, whom you know, whom you like
well enough, who are kind to you, and who are a
sort of friend, yet would you go to one of them in
your sorrow? would you go to one of them to tell
your boyish griefs, and ask for the word of advice
in your doubt? would you feel sure of a kindly
look, of an attentive ear, of exactly the medicine

for your disease, by going to such an one? If so, he is a true friend. Oh, sympathy is one of the dearest gifts of GOD to us. Cannot you remember how in your younger days you would go to your mother and tell her your little trials and troubles, big enough to you, and look up in her face for help, in perfect faith that she could give it? Did you not know that the kind expression would come into that face and that the smile of tender sympathy would be lent to your petition? Have you no such friend to whom you feel you would not appeal in vain, none with whom you yearn to meet, and to tell all your heart out? If you find such friends, grapple them to your hearts with hoops of steel, make much of them, bear with their weaknesses, for they are witnesses of the love of JESUS CHRIST in this world.

And then lastly, if to some of you such friendship is a blank, a thing unknown; if it has not been yours to feel that magic instinct of love and sympathy for a friend which betrays itself in a look, a smile, a touch; if the story of David and Jonathan is a story in which you feel you have no part or lot, still do not feel alone, for still to you there may be a "Friend Who sticketh closer than a brother," and that Friend is CHRIST. "I have trodden the wine-press alone," said the Man CHRIST JESUS, "and of the people there was none with Me." Whom on earth could JESUS call His friend in the sense which I have been describing to you?

G

Alone He seemed to tread the ways of the world, and if we know the value of a friend to be beyond all price, and the loss of a friend to be outside words, did not our great Friend Himself never yearn for sympathy, think you, and the love of His fellow-men?  Oh that love, that sympathy, that friendship of CHRIST!  He loved, not as we do, coldly, imperfectly, with a love greater than can embrace but a few; His ocean of love embraced mankind; no one so fallen, so poor, so sad, but His love surrounded them with its full tide of tenderness.    Yet we have the touch of human craving for sympathy mixed with the trustfulness in His FATHER in the cry, "Ye shall leave Me alone, and yet I am not alone, because the FATHER is with Me."

Oh, no! you can never be alone if CHRIST is with you.   Here you may never know what friendship, and love, and sympathy truly mean.   You may see, and it is perhaps a bitter thing to see in other families, in other boys, in those you fain would love, a deep abiding love, and with it bright happiness, and a beauty, beyond your grasp, yet

> "Trust in GOD,
> And borrow ease for heart and mind."

Perhaps the fault lies in you, perhaps you are not unselfish enough, perhaps you won't give up what you think your due to others.   I can hardly imagine that any one would like to have no real friend; yet remember, if God is for you, it matters little who is against you. Tell all your griefs and trials to Him, go to Him, not as a dreadful Judge, a stern Ruler, but as a loving and tender Friend, and He will wipe away all tears from your eyes, and be a strong tower of refuge in all your trouble.

Believe me, friendship is a beautiful and lovely thing. Do not abuse it, do not substitute an imitation for the reality, do not be ashamed of it : we are all toiling slowly and painfully along the valley of life, and climbing the great cliff of eternity. Do not leave your brother behind, bring him to Christ, help him to surmount the sharp crags and stones of temptation and sin by your words of kindness, and by substantial help. So in that land which seems to you now so very far off, you will stand on the top of this cliff that now looks so high, in the presence of your God, not alone, but with those whom you have loved and sympathised with on earth.

"For ever with the Lord,
Amen, so let it be."

———

## X.

## HANDWRITINGS.

*" In the same hour came forth fingers of a man's hand, and wrote over against the candlestick upon the plaister of the wall of the king's palace, and the king saw the part of the hand that wrote."*—Daniel v. 5.

I WISH you first of all to think what the scene was which the prophet Daniel wrote about in these words. The great city of Babylon was being besieged by the army of the Persian prince Cyrus, and the walls were so thick and high that the Persians could not get inside to take it. The King Belshazzar thought himself quite safe, and had ordered a great banquet to be prepared, and a feast to be given to his chief courtiers and captains. There they all are before us feasting and revelling, drinking wine out of the vessels which they had brought out of the temple of GOD at Jerusalem, and were now using for their own profane or common use. The king himself has dismissed all fear of the enemy from his mind ; and all have given themselves up to the enjoyment of the present festivity.

Hundreds of lights gleam from the gilded ceiling, and the sound of revelry makes the vast hall resound with gaiety and tumult. Yet, had they but known it, outside in the darkness a very dif-

ferent scene is going on. Along the dry bed of
the river Euphrates, the waters of which had been
turned away into another channel, were stealing
the Persian soldiers under their leader Cyrus, soon
to break in upon the crowd of unarmed revellers
and seize the kingdom for themselves.

The feasting is at its highest—when suddenly
upon the walls of the hall appear gigantic fingers,
as of a man's hand, which slowly trace out awful
characters upon the wall. And as the letters stand
out thereon in all their terrible grandeur, dismay
and terror fall upon all hearts ! None can read the
writing, and all they know is, that some mysterious
warning is given them, but what the danger is
coming upon them, they cannot say.

Now, boys, you perhaps wonder what this has
to do with you, and how this strange ghostly handwriting on the walls of this palace, thousands of
years ago, can affect you, who sit here before me.
I will try and show you, that for you too, very
young as almost all of you are, GOD writes at
times in handwriting which is so plain and so clear
that " he who runs may read," so large that the
smallest and youngest child can see the letters.
Let us try for a few moments to think when GOD's
handwriting is thus shown to us.

First, then, though at all times GOD is speaking
to us, yet there are certain times and seasons when
He seems to come closer to us, and when we draw
near to Him. When we lie on the bed of sickness,

and have leisure to think over our life, our faults, our errors ; when the busy life outside seems withdrawn awhile from us, GOD then comes very near us, and this handwriting is plainer in these hours of illness, when the memory of past events casts its shadow over our soul, than in the daily business of life. Only let us all beware lest, when we once again are strong and vigorous, and breathe again the full glow of health, when all seems joyous and happy around us ; we must beware then lest we forget our good intentions, and so GOD's handwriting become fainter and fainter.

Or, again. GOD sometimes snatches away from us some one who was very dear and near to us ; some father, mother, brother, sister, or friend, on whom we relied, whose advice we valued, whom we respected, admired, loved. There seems to us when very young at such times a blank so big that nothing can fill it up : we recall sadly everything, however trifling, said, looked, or done by our dear one gone away from us. At such a time GOD's handwriting is very plain before us, bidding us turn to Him, and to Him alone, for help in time of need, saying to us that such an one is not lost, but only gone before us, that our life here must not be so wrapt up in earthly love, that GOD is put in a second place ; and yet the handwriting is full of mercy and tender love, for it whispers to us that after this life ended we shall see again those who have left us,

" And with the morn those angel faces smile,
Which we have loved long since and lost awhile."

I have seen once a terrible railway accident, one of the very worst, perhaps, which has happened the last thirty years or so. It was on Christmas Eve, and no one could look on those lying dead there amid the snow, in numbers, hurled in a minute into their Creator's presence, without thinking that here was a message from GOD to those who saw it. "Remember thy Creator in the days of thy youth, when the evil days come not."

And yet once more. GOD speaks to us often on particular occasions of less striking moment. When you come back to school, at the beginning of a new term, when you make resolutions to live better than you have done, to conquer old faults, to do your duty, to obey cheerfully those over you, to put aside all ill-temper, untruthfulness, and indolence ; that is a more than ordinary time. Or again, at the end of a term, when you go to a new and bigger school ; when you are launched out upon a larger sea of school life, when new temptations that you now know nothing of come upon you; that is a more than ordinary time. But there are many, very many others. A letter from home, a word, or even a look of advice, the words of a hymn or a book ; these all may be the handwritings of GOD to your young hearts. One handwriting there is that you must never neglect— and that is, prayer. Every night and morning, as you kneel by your bedside, be sure you make that a time of special influence, of special help, of special grace to yourselves.    GOD is then of all times most near to you.    He then talks to you face to face. Do not let such times go by without rising from your knees, feeling that you have gained some inward strength, that like Jacob of old you have wrestled with GOD and prevailed.    There is nothing in this world that can take the place of prayer.    " More things are wrought by prayer than this world dreams of," says a very great poet And, believe me, if you neglect your prayers, if you feel when you say them that there is a mist, a something between you and your FATHER in Heaven ; if you have gained nothing of help and comfort from one prayer only, then you will be sure not to live well, and wisely, and happily, during the week.

GOD forbid that I should by any word of mine throw a cloud over the sunshine of your young hearts.    But, if you learn, now that you are young, before the evil days come upon you, to read GOD's handwriting at all times, you will not be like the wicked king and his courtiers, who fell that night at the hand of the Persians, unable to read GOD's warning and unconscious of their fate.    Rather, if from your childhood you have at all times tried to see GOD's message and to read it aright, if you have watched for such writing and expected your LORD's coming, will you as you go through life be

ready, and armed against all assaults, and then may
GOD grant to you one and all

> " That having all things done,
> And all your conflicts past,
> Ye may o'ercome through CHRIST alone,
> And perfect stand at last."

---

## XI.

## CHARACTER.

*" All the rivers run into the sea."*—Eccles. i. 7.

YOU all, or nearly all, have seen the sea, you have
perhaps seen him like an infant sleeping peacefully,
and have watched the blue waves gleaming and
dancing in the warm sunlight; as they crept lazily
upon the beach one after the other. You have perhaps seen him in his gigantic fury, lashing himself
wildly along, threatening to swallow up all obstacles,
and to shatter the flimsy boats that ride upon his
surface. Among the Greeks and Romans, the God
of the sea, the earth-shaker, Neptune, was held in
high honour, and was of equal dignity with Jupiter or
Zeus himself. His palace was thought to be in
the depth of the sea, where he kept his horses with
brazen hoofs and golden manes; as he rode in his
chariot, driving his steeds, the waters became calm,
the heaving bosom of the deep afforded a level highway for its Lord and Master.

I think the first idea of the sea which we feel, is its immense size. The waters thereof stretch as far as eye can reach, and you feel this much more after going through a great river, as little by little the land recedes from view, and at length the liquid surface is on all sides; and the great river upon which you are sailing on slowly into the greater sea—Whence comes it? What is its home?

Do you see that little fountain far away, bubbling up amid green rushes, the little lake on whose surface lie the water lilies in their beauty of white and green, the brook that bubbles along to-day as for hundreds of years amid green fields, whose banks are laden with forget-me-nots, and many a flower? How slowly and quietly the little brook steals along in its course, yet it grows bigger and bigger as we pursue its course, and large towns take the place of the green fields, and wharves and buildings form its new banks now. Man plies his busy work on its bosom, and boats and ships move up and down it. Can this broad mighty stream be the grown up offspring of the little fountain, the little lake, the scarcely moving brook, the infant born so many hundreds of miles away? yes, it is; so do the rivers run towards the sea.

And is not the meaning of the words used by the wisest man, King Solomon, plain to us? Alike in body, in mind, and in spirit, our river of life moves towards the great sea of eternity. We cannot moor our boat here or there to land. We cannot go back, we are hurried along GOD knows whither, towards the great ocean where all is for ever lost in the dim horizon of faith. Yes, my dear boys, you cannot go back, you cannot live over again your yesterday, you cannot recall that thought or act done yesterday, done last week, last year, many many years ago. And I want to talk to you to-night of the importance of *habit* which bears such fruit in your body, your mind, and your spirit.

First then in your body. Are you not all aware how much habits do for you? If you wish to be able to play a game well, must you not practise it? To attain success in any bodily feat or dexterity, habit or practice is essential for nearly all, and even those few who are born players, so to speak, can much improve themselves by attention to the game. Take for instance, such a man as Blondin who has walked across the Falls of Niagara on a rope. Do you think that he all at once jumped into the position of being able to walk at a dazzling height? You see him so high, looking so much at his ease, but you do not see, and you know nothing of the years in his childhood of hard work, and doubtless frequent failure. It is true that of the three parts of man, the body, mind, and spirit, the body is much the lowest; yet it is GOD's handiwork, and therefore we ought not to neglect it, but ought rather to maintain and improve its excellence. Therefore in your bodies, I would say, strive for the mastery, and practise that by habits of steady perseverance you may gain this mastery.

And secondly, if this is true of the body, it is no less true of that far nobler part of us, the mind; the two often go together, though not always. It is the prayer of the Roman poet, Horace, to be given a "mens sana in corpore sano," a sound mind in a sound body. Let me take an example or two of the force of habit. The present Premier of England, Lord Beaconsfield, is a noble example of how habits tend to make the man's character, how practice makes perfect. He started with no peculiar advantage in life, and from being of Jewish origin, was perhaps exposed more than others to thoughtless dislike and contempt. When he made his first speech in the House of Commons, the members of it laughed openly, and were for hissing him down. "The day will come when you shall hear me," said the young orator, and he set himself to alter his faults of speaking, to remedy mistakes of manner and the like, and he has risen now to be the first man in England, and to occupy a very prominent feature in the future history of the world. His is a grand history of hard honest work and splendid industry, (I use the words advisedly) splendidly rewarded. Take the example of a great actor. There is a hush before he enters; all eyes are directed idly on those on the stage, for they are so eager to welcome their favourite. He comes forward, and is received with immense applause.

How carefully he uses his voice, how every attitude, every gesture, every whisper is studied! He is not *acting* Hamlet, he *is* Hamlet. Yes! but then think what years of toil and burning the midnight oil, and study of the author have gradually raised him to this pitch of excellence. Depend upon it, this perfection has been slowly and painfully attained; he has had to learn and unlearn, to cut out this, and to introduce that, to compare one way with another way, to give up some favourite action, and to adopt one disagreeable to his feelings. I know for certain, that perhaps the greatest actor of the present day, Mr. Henry Irving, after acting in Shakespeare's masterpieces, goes from the theatre to his club in London and reads over his Shakespeare with all its different readings and comments, till the grey light of morning surprises him. His success is largely due to habit. It is the same with the author, the poet, the painter, the sculptor. The world sees the result, and judges rightly by the result. Those verses that glide along so smoothly, and in such simple guise, that picture so true to nature that every blade of grass and even pebble stands out sharply and clearly, that book that seems so true to your own feelings as you read it, so full of thoughts that of themselves create a new world of thought in your mind, that sculpture so grand, and yet truthfully expressing every muscle and ligament of the body—these one and all have been hewn out of hard rock, chiselled and wrought to perfection by much study and working up of detail, and a habit formed of careful work.

And you know this to be the case yourselves in your daily work. When you begin a new lesson, say such a new language as Greek, you know nothing, the letters appear to you of no meaning, yet they are symbols of the language, and without mastering the alphabet and working through the more dry details of grammar, you can never come out upon the real beauties and rich treasures of Greek literature.

And thirdly, is not this true of our spirit, our noblest, our most divine part? How truly does all experience show that here "the rivers run into the sea." Think each of you, young as you are, how far your daily thoughts, words, and acts have made you what you are. Each one of you started equal in the race of life. Each one was baptised and made a member of CHRIST, a child of GOD, and an inheritor of the kingdom of Heaven. Each one of you, I take it, has learnt to pray and to know for yourself with that blessed instinct which GOD has given to childhood, "whatsoever things are good, whatsoever things are pure, whatsoever things are lovely, if there be any praise, and if there be any virtue, think on these things." There needs no prophet from GOD, no teacher, to tell you for yourselves that there is a great gulf fixed between right and wrong. GOD's Holy Spirit guides you into all truth; GOD's holy angels encamp around you,

CHARACTER.

your father and mother, those older and wiser than you, shield you from harm and surround you with all good and holy influence, yet the day must come, as to Adam in the paradise of Eden, when temptation falls upon you. Your goodness hitherto is no merit to you, for evil has been carefully kept from sight; you leave home for school, and there you find new temptations or old temptations put in a new form.

Let us go more into detail; for a sermon is nothing if not likely to bear practical fruit. You come here fresh from home, and you have learnt to pray; your prayers have been something real to you; you have not merely made a form of them, but they have been times, however rare and short, set apart from common use, and dedicated to GOD's service. In your prayers you have found comfort and sympathy; you have been helped forward to bear misunderstandings, disappointments, and sorrows; you have risen from your knees lighter in heart, and feeling that you have successfully asked GOD for forgiveness for the past, and grace to meet new trials and temptations. Have you ever felt this? · And then perhaps, you know not how or when, for the beginning of slipping away from good habits cannot always be remembered, you said your prayers with other thoughts prying as intruders into this most Holy of Holies; you missed part of them, or you were hurried over them, and slowly the relief, the sympathy, the

grace of prayer dies away. Do you think I speak
too strongly of this habit? Oh, no! for I believe
that if you pray aright, you will live aright. I
would say, Never give up the habit, even if you
only pray with your heart; the outward form of
kneeling by your bedside may mean little or nothing, yet by GOD's means it may recall a memory
of better days, and it is better than to fling yourself
down to sleep—a sleep unblest by GOD, and un-
guarded by the ministering angels who hover round
you. Therefore I beg of you, never let slip the
habit of prayer; it is so hard to recover the habit
if once lost; it is so hard to find GOD again in
prayer, when once deserted. It is impossible for
any of you to walk with GOD in this life, and to
see your FATHER in Heaven hereafter, if you give
up this habit of prayer.

And another habit I will insist upon as only
second is *unselfishness*. Have you never felt a
thrill of happiness pass through you when you
have given to another genuine pleasure, and have
really denied yourself something, however small,
that another may gain and be the happier? O do
think of this, and practise it in your week-day life.
Those of you who are older and stronger, give up
what you like to the weaker; do it cheerfully, and
the *effort* of it will soon pass away. This is a very
hard habit to form; and to form a habit of selfishness is so very easy and natural. I know how hard
a habit this is, and so I do urge you; do not

simply sit here and think, " now I will give up my
own will and my own pleasure," but put it into
practice. It is more blessed to give than to receive, for so, little by little, you will learn that
more happiness even in this world comes from
self-denial in little everyday things—what they are,
you well know yourselves—than from living as the
rich man in the parable, careless of others, and
only anxious to get all the good out of life for
himself. Oh, it would give me more pleasure and
happiness to see you try really, try honestly, try to
remember this lesson, than anything else you can
do. For this spirit of unselfishness is the most
beautiful rose in the bouquet of Christian virtue.
It may not always be the sign of a life at one with
GOD. The outward shell of it was seen in the
death of a most unchristian King, Charles II.,
who on his death-bed turned to his courtiers, and
begged them with exquisite courtesy to excuse
him for having been so long a time dying. The
real kernel was seen alike in the life and death of
one of the noblest saints of GOD that ever lived,
whose life I hope some day all you boys will read,
Charles Kingsley. A friend of his writes of him :
" One day seeing him quit his work to busy himself in some slight matter for me, I asked him not
to trouble about it then and there, and he turning
upon me with unusual warmth, said, ' Trouble ! don't
talk to me of that, or you will make me angry, I
never allow myself to think about trouble.' In the

hour of death his daughter heard him exclaim, 'How beautiful GOD is,' true to his own words written long before, 'Self should be forgotten most of all in the hour of death.'"

Yes, and lastly, cultivate the habit of manliness, by which I mean, frame a habit of doing what is good, and pure, and GOD-like; saying a word for GOD, and good and truth against wrong. If you hear, and see, and join in, what is base and low and wrong, little by little your character must become more feeble for good, more prone to evil. True manliness is not ashamed of weakness or poverty, or unpopularity. GOD give you all this true *virtus*, this manliness of chivalry, so noble, so loving, so beautiful. Do not think, I will join in this wrong thing because every one else does; do not say, I do not see much harm in that wrong thing because others do it. You will then be unmanly cowards, and sailing with the stream, will drift out into the sea of an evil and weak character.

Such a character was not that of this true knight of JESUS CHRIST, of whom I have just spoken. He had faults may be of temper and hastiness; he was impatient perhaps of restraint, and at times his foot slipped; yet by daily habit, as surely as rivers run into the sea, so surely did his life become prayerful, unselfish, manly. O do try to imitate such a life, try in your play, in your work, in your intercourse with one another, and with us here, and with those at home, to raise up by slow degrees a life founded on the rock of daily principle, not merely on the sand of occasional good intention : so will you come like Charles Kingsley both to live and die the death of the righteous, so will your last days be like his.

"Who," says a great writer there, " can forget that funeral on the 28th of January, 1875, and the large and sad throng that gathered round his grave ! There was the representative of the Prince of Wales, and close by the gipsies of Eversley Common. There was the Squire of his village, and the labourers young and old, officers and sailors, the bishop of his diocese, and the dean of his abbey, peers and members of the House of Commons, authors and publishers, and the huntsmen in pink, —for though as good a clergyman as any, Charles Kingsley had been a good sportsman, and has taken in his life many a fence as bravely as he took the last fence of all, without fear or trembling. . . . . All went home, feeling that life was poorer, and every one knew that he had lost a friend who had been in some peculiar sense his own."

## XII.

## RESULTS.

*" Cast thy bread upon the waters, for thou shalt find it after many days."*—Ecclesiastes xi. 1.

PERHAPS no man in this generation has exercised a wider influence, at least over school life, than Thomas Arnold, Head Master of Rugby, and in pausing for a few moments to-night to set before ourselves the picture of this great man, we must remember that the schools of England were then as different from what they are now as darkness from light.

He first taught that lesson that the lives of those who teach and those who are taught should not be lives of mutual suspicion and dislike, but of love and of sympathy, of quiet duty and obedience, and mutual self-respect ; that love and respect need not, and ought not, to be foes to each other. "Is this a Christian school?" was his indignant question, when once a very bad feeling had been displayed among his boys : "I cannot remain here if all is to be carried on by restraint and force; if I am to be here as gaoler, I will resign my office at once." And at another time, when owing to a rebellious spirit several boys had been expelled, standing up in the great school, he said in that deep ringing voice of his, "It is not necessary that this

school should be a school of three hundred or one
hundred, or of fifty boys, but it *is* necessary that it
should be a school of *Christian gentlemen.*" To
take an instance of his then new treatment of boys,
he placed entire confidence in a boy's word. "If
you say so," he would say quickly, "that is quite
enough, of course I believe your word." Hence
there arose a strong feeling in Rugby school, that
it was a shame to tell Arnold a lie, he always be.
lieved one. And on Sunday it was his delight to
advise, comfort and warn his young audience for a
week's and life's work by a few brief words. There
are hundreds now living who recall that scene of
his labours which he so loved to occupy. There,
Sunday after Sunday, he stood up and pleaded for
his LORD, pleaded earnestly on behalf of godliness,
purity, unselfishness, and all that is noble and
lovely in this life. And, writes one of his boys,
now a Member of Parliament, "we listened, as all
boys in their better moods will listen, to a man
whom we *felt* to be with all his heart and soul and
strength, striving against whatever was mean and
unmanly, and wrong in our little world." And so,
wearily, and little by little, was brought home to
the young boy for the first time the meaning of his
life; that it was no fool's or sluggard's paradise
into which he had wandered by chance, but a
battlefield where even the youngest must take his
side, and the stakes are life and death. And thus
throughout his whole life,—too short, alas, for the

work on hand,—he laboured unceasingly for the good, and against the evil, till "GOD's finger touched him, and he slept." What a blank was there in the life of many of those who had known him from boyhood, and learnt to love him dearly ; how they felt that a strong rock of defence was suddenly removed from their midst, that never again should they turn to him for comfort in their trouble, counsel in the hour of need, a helping hand ever ready to grasp them and lead them nearer GOD, on the road of eternal life. Yes, the autumn evening descends, and across the dim fields falls the brief November day ; out come the lights in the schoolroom windows, the withered leaves are falling slowly in troops from the great elms, but man is gone to his long home. Yet grieve not as those without hope, for indeed the memory of the just is blessed ; that strong great spirit lives on in blessed memories, in the good and holy lives of those who as boys rested under the boughs of that mighty oak.

Is not his a life to imitate ? Surely it is. A life of which his son has written :

> " Thou would'st not alone
> Be saved, my father ! alone
> Conquer and come to thy goal,
> Leaving the rest in the wild.
>
>     ＊      ＊      ＊      ＊
>
> Therefore to thee it was given
> Many to save with thyself,

And at the end of the day, come,
O faithful shepherd, come,
Bringing thy sheep in thy hand.
And through thee I believe
In the noble and great who are gone,
Servants of GOD, or sons,
Shall I not call you ?"

Yes, boys, Thomas Arnold has not in vain cast his bread upon the waters, for he being dead yet speaketh with a voice that has made the schools of England the noble places that in the main, with all their faults, they are—one of the glories of England whence her sons go forth into the battle of life, we trust many of them

" Strong in the strength which GOD supplies,"

to meet, fight, and overcome the temptations of the world, the flesh, and the devil.

To-night, let us muse, away from ourselves, out of this quiet life of ours, for a little space, and think of the ways in which men cast their bread upon the waters : remembering this always, that *we* may plant and sow and water the seed, but only GOD can give the increase.

" We plough the fields and scatter
The good seed on the land ;
But it is fed and watered
By GOD's Almighty hand."

Look at the life of a clergyman among the dens and alleys of a large town parish, where in the

burden and heat of the day he must be ever ready
to be a father in GOD to those in his parish, counting all things but loss, and careless of his own
comfort and wants, so only he may bring souls to
CHRIST.   There are many such whose lives seem
hidden away; they never gain fame, and attain
glory or riches; yet such are truly fishers of men,
and are casting the bread of life upon the waters
of struggling misery and wickedness.   Their lives
are hidden, but they are hidden on every side with
CHRIST.

Or, again, take the life of a missionary in a far
distant land.   He has perhaps at GOD's call like
Abraham, given up home, fatherland and all.   He
has bidden good-bye to his nearest and dearest in
life, to all his bright hopes and prospects of success, to work in a land of strangers, in a new
climate, amid men and women who worship igno-
rantly and falsely.   He has obeyed his Master's
call when He called to him; when he heard the
SAVIOUR say, "Follow Me," even to a life of unceasing toil and the death of the cross, "he
arose, and followed Him."   Such are labourers in
CHRIST's vineyard, of whom it is written in the
beautiful words of Isaiah, "Blessed are ye that
sow beside all waters, that send forth thither the feet
of the ox and the ass."   And our text reads a
lesson to all such, whoever they are, wherever they
may be, young or old, teachers or taught, that
there's ne'er a soul so black but it may struggle

back to purer hopes, and wash its sins in JESUS'
Blood. Should we say of any one of the creatures
whom GOD has made, "He is hopeless, he has
again and again broken the laws of GOD and man,
he must go his own way, we can do no more?"
Nay, but O man, who art thou that judgest another?
Remember, GOD seeth not as man seeth. That
boy whom you deem always in fault, who is always
being punished, and who has no one's good word,
was made of GOD; GOD loves him, his guardian
angel loves him. Toil, labour, work, and though
you may never see it, believe that you are not all
in vain casting your bread upon the waters. And
to-night, on this last Sunday of term, it is well for
us every one to review our life of the term, and to
see for ourselves whether the bread of life, the fruit
of an earnest and real seeking after GOD, is growing in our lives, into I do not say *perfection*, but
into a change of life, and a closer walk with GOD.

The life of a schoolmaster is one that must ever,
or ought to be ever, casting bread upon the waters.
It has its sorrows and its joys. For we who are
over you and lead you must ever have our disappointments at your failures and your slips into sin;
disappointments that you know little of, and better
so. We may have struggled, yes, and prayed to
GOD, to make you turn from that particular sin of
idleness, untruthfulness, selfishness, anger; yet
after so many words of warning, you fall back again
into the old paths. And further, it must ever be

in school life, that we lose sight after awhile of
you. You go from us into the bigger life of a
bigger school, and hence into the great world beyond, and we may never see you more on this side
the grave, and may be you will forget us, and your
life here, though not always, I hope. Yet herein
lies a thought of comfort; for hereafter, in that
land where GOD and His dear angels are, in that
blessed home beyond the skies, we may meet and
know each other. And if we by one word, or one
act of ours, have furthered you on the way to GOD,
if we have taught you, however imperfectly, as
indeed must needs be, but still as best we might,
to hold fast that which is good ; to set before you
a dim, imperfect standard of what you should be,
to pray aright, to speak the truth, to lead the lives
of Christian boys, O then we are repaid a thousandfold. And we must ask ourselves, Have we done
our duty to you? have we striven to be just in
our punishments, stern against the sin, yet loving
to the sinner? full of sympathy to sorrow, more
strict to ourselves than to you ? Truly we need to
say in the words of the hymn,

> " Give those who teach pure hearts and wise,
>     Faith, hope, and love, all warmed by prayer ;
> Themselves first training for the skies,
>     They best will train their people there."

And on your side, look over the account of your
term. Have you profited by this term ? First,

then, are you able to say you have learnt anything in your work? Have you a clearer insight into it, and have you tried to do your best in your lessons? Your parents have sent you here partly that you may become wiser and learn : we labour as best we can to teach you what we know. How is your account in this respect? And yet again, how is the account of your spiritual talents? Can you put your finger on any one darling sin, and say, "By God's help I have striven against this sin, and I think I have got the better of it? Have you tried to be kinder and less selfish in little daily acts? Have you found a new meaning in prayer, and a reality in God's service which was not there before? Can you honestly say that through all your slips and shortcomings, all your forgetfulness of God, and the wishes of those who care for you and pray for you, yet that you have gained a little of that spirit of CHRIST, and tasted the happiness and inward peace which can only be in the purest and best sense to those who love God and follow His commandments? You on your side should one and all pray with heart and soul,

> " Give those who learn the willing ear,
> The spirit meek, the guileless mind ;
> Such gifts will make the lowliest here
> Far better than a kingdom find."

You are going home for your holidays—well earned holidays, I feel sure, I know, for many of you ; do not think that larger liberty means larger licence ; do not live one life here, another at home. You will be among other friends and companions ; you will be also among other temptations. Do not think for one moment that we grudge you one hour or one minute of your happiness ; nay, in the best sense of the word, we wish you " God speed," but I for one should be sorry indeed that in your home life you should forget the lessons which you have learnt of unselfishness, love, forbearance, self-denial, putting away of temper and wrong thoughts. Oh, I beg you, do not forget these. Let those at home who love you so dearly and so well see with pleasure that you are more considerate to them in their wishes, more kind and ready to give up to your brothers and sisters ; less given to sullen looks and angry moods, and conceit and thoughts of self. Do you think this means a loss of holiday? Believe me, no. You will find in the love of others, and in inward happiness, a new holiday that you knew not of,—and we who have watched over you in our little way shall feel we have not cast our bread upon the waters in vain.

Thus labouring, ever all of us learning the lessons our great Master Christ has taught us ; ever looking to Him as our Guide and Teacher ; ever counting ourselves to know nothing, and as children in the eyes of our great Father, we shall at length reach our endless holiday, when the term of life is over, and we exchange the school of life for the home of GOD's Paradise in Heaven. Should not we, if we truly seek that better land, if we would do our duty in this life, if we would be ready to meet our GOD, ever pray in the words of the hymn?

" O bless the shepherd, bless the sheep,
 That guide and guided both be one,
One in the faithful watch they keep,
 Until this hurrying life be done."

---

## XIII.

## THE INNER LIFE.

*"What, could ye not watch with Me one hour?"*—S. Matt. xxvi. 40.

IT is even-tide, and the sun has sunk to his rest over the Mount of Olivet. The great Temple with its marble pillars and stately grandeur, stands out cold and clear under the pale light of the moon, peeping through the trees of the garden of Gethsemane. The waters of the brook Kedron prattle along in the still air of evening, and the scene is one of rest and solemnity. Can it be that in a few short hours the city that sleeps so nigh will be mad with the tumult of Jews clamouring for CHRIST's blood? Can it be that this very hour the SON of GOD will be betrayed and de-

livered into the hands of wicked men? Can it be
that a brief day will see a nation setting at nought
their SAVIOUR,—a world crucifying the LORD of
Life?

How calm looks that city of towers, "that sweet
city with her dreaming spires," the earthly Jerusa-
lem, the joy of the whole earth. Perchance our
SAVIOUR is looking back on it with sorrow as He
enters this garden,—a favourite resort of His,—with
His three chosen ones, Peter, James, and John.
If so, be assured, "more in sorrow than in anger."
Even now the band of conspirators, with Judas
Iscariot at their head, are stealing through the
trees, bent on the foul design of seizing the de-
fenceless JESUS. Alone He wrestles in prayer with
GOD His FATHER in that last dread hour of agony.
Yes, in the valley of death, into the lengthening
shadows of night, He must enter alone. "I have
trodden the wine-press alone, and of the people
there was none with Me." Yet even in this anguish
of soul He yearns for human sympathy, and we
feel His tone of sorrow in the words of the text,
spoken to His sleeping Apostle, "What, could ye
not watch one hour?"

Boys, I wish you to-night, at the beginning of
a new term, to lay before you this message of
CHRIST,—"Watch with Me one hour." *One hour?*
Is it too much? Is *one hour* much in all lifetime?
And yet for the loss of that one hour, you may
lose the eternal Presence of GOD, and the heaven

prepared for those who watch on earth. For the gain of that one hour you may exchange the weary watching into everlasting sight of GOD and of the Lamb.

And I cannot proceed to tell you what seem hindrances and helps in the way of spending this one hour watching with JESUS, without calling your attention to this fact,—that even the Son of Man, possessed of the deepest anguish of soul, even when GOD hid as it were His face from Him, yet turned and yearned for human sympathy. And surely He had a right to look for such sympathy from His Apostles, from a human point of view. Alike in the dusty streets of the city, and the barren wastes of Galilee, by the sea coast, and on the hill top, He had comforted them, led them, sympathised with them, advised them,—He had led them tenderly, as a shepherd leadeth his sheep. If He had bidden them partake of the water of affliction, He had given them the bread of life for sustenance. Yet He looks in vain. His chosen three,—one of them that beloved Apostle who leaned on His breast at the last Supper, whom JESUS loved,—all have not understood the depth of the SAVIOUR'S woe. The zealous Peter and the enthusiastic sons of Zebedee sleep, while their GOD and their Friend looks to them for a word of sympathy.

Let us now for a few moments turn to ourselves, and look at some of the causes which make us like the three Apostles fast asleep, when Jesus looks towards us.

First then, you are young, and life is all stretched out before you. You have seen a brook with its stepping-stones set in order across the babbling waters, in order to aid the traveller crossing. You have as yet in your life few stepping-stones where you may stand, and resting look back. Your leaving home to come here was a stepping-stone. It was, or ought to have been, a time of peculiar pause to each of you. Home influence, home affection, a father's, a mother's tenderness, these are for awhile taken from you, and you enter into a new society. The wrench may be slighter or greater, according to circumstances and your own feelings, but you are (whether you are aware of it or no) crossing on to a new stepping-stone across the brook of life. Still you are young, you can set before your mind in the future your going hence into a bigger school, and thence, after years perhaps, out into the still bigger school of life. And then—and then— Will you not, though you are so young, spare *one* hour of youth to God? It is true that, humanly speaking, you have many years to live,—that you are but just opening your eyes to God's world,—that your time of life is one of sunshine. Yet time slips away so fast, and the present passes even in a breath. It seems but yesterday to the grown man or woman that they were sitting at their mother's knee, listening to the hymn for children; that they were sitting round the Christmas fire full of life and spirits, listening to the fairy stories, never tired as they listened to them, and their wise father's voice, as they played on the golden sands of childhood, heedless, thoughtless, innocent. But it is not yesterday,—it is years and years ago, and they are grown up, and—well, GOD perchance has been very good to them. No, you in your youth think you can ill spare one hour for GOD. And why so? Let us look, and we shall find the answer.

Well, we say, we have so many calls on our time; we have so much to do; there is Sunday to be good in. Surely one day out of seven is enough to *give up* to goodness and to GOD. Besides, we do say our prayers night and morning.

But I say distinctly, No, this will not do,—this is not enough.

The age of boyhood bears with it, I take it, an *instinct of religion*, by which I mean, that all children by nature have a desire, yes, I will say a yearning, after what is good, noble, and holy. But many things may go to blunt this instinct. Picture your life, had you been born in misery in the poor fever-stricken streets of some large town, with vice surrounding you on every side, with no words of comfort or of better things, hopeless and godless. Or again, without being reared in an atmosphere of miserable sin, you may be brought up

I

among people who have no care for GOD, and the
things of GOD.   They are not ill livers,—they do
not steal, or lie, or swear; they may go to church
at times, and appear outwardly respectable members of society,—*but yet* you grow up without any
good principles in your heart implanted by home
teaching, and simply dependent on your surround-
ings and your companions as to whether you will
serve GOD in this life or no.

But you, I trust, have not so learned CHRIST.
You have happy homes, dear friends, those around
you who, however themselves away from GOD,
would dearly wish you to become followers of
CHRIST in your lives.   But then you have your
work, your play, and the thousand things which
are always occurring to distract your mind,—and
these things step in between you and thoughts of
GOD and holy things.

Now I agree so far, that it is very hard,—I will
go so far as to say impossible, for you to be constantly thinking over holy and sacred hopes and
aims.   You have your daily life to live, a life of
activity which admits few minutes for secret communion with your FATHER in Heaven; but this I
would urge upon you, Do not let anything whatever prevent your watching *one hour* with CHRIST.
And if you ask me what this means, I will very
briefly try and show you.

GOD takes you even now, young as you are, at
times out of the high road of daily routine duty

into the Garden of Gethsemane, there to watch
with Him, it may be for one hour.

> "There is a secret place of rest,
>     GOD's saints alone may know,
> Thou shalt not find it east or west,
>     Though seeking to and fro ;
> A cell where JESUS is the door,
>     His love the only key ;
> Who enter will go out no more,
>     But there with JESUS be."
>                             *Inner Life.*

Is that *inner life* a mystery to you,—a something
you know not of? Do you stand outside the
Garden of Gethsemane with the many? It is not
by mere emotion, by good feelings of a moment,
by the impression of a hymn or a sermon, or so
forth ; not by saying, "LORD, LORD," that we
gain admittance into that garden where CHRIST is.
No, we must carry our professions into actions,
—we must take CHRIST with us in our lessons,
our play, our daily life. We must in the dress of
workers live the life of heroes, we must walk along
every inch of the long white dusty road of daily
duty. You have no doubt heard of the monks
of old time. There are men now who think and
act very much as they did. They went out of the
world and dwelt by themselves in the desert or in
convents where they might think on nought but
holy things, and might shut out (as they thought)
the world, the flesh and the devil. But this was

not CHRIST'S way.   We need not be *of* the world, but we must be *in* the world.

My dear boys, set yourselves this term in earnest to spend *one hour* in this manner with CHRIST. You need make no outward professions, you need not be quoting religious expressions, you need not make long prayers,—but in your life among yourselves, with us, here, and at home, so act as children of GOD.   You will not be less happy; you will be more happy.   You will not feel a sense of sadness ever present in your daily pursuits, but GOD will hallow all you think or do.   Away from Him who can be safe?   Not the wisest or strongest in this world but must come like little children to spend their hour of life with CHRIST, if they would taste the truest happiness on earth, and reach the eternal happiness of Heaven.

And lastly,—Only in Him, only apart from outer things, and alone with CHRIST in the Garden of Gethsemane can you find the *perfect sympathy*. To *watch* is an order, and it implies a degree of loneliness.   And to shrink from GOD'S order argues weakness, however natural.   The cry of the Psalmist, " Oh that I had wings like a dove, for then would I flee away and be at rest," is not the highest faith.   Higher and more perfect, and not beyond our reach, is the prayer uttered in the garden of CHRIST, " Not My will, but Thine be done."   He best follows the SON of GOD JESUS CHRIST, who hugs the Cross to his breast, and who sheds tears of agony with Him in Gethsemane.

All you prize most highly here, all you hold dearest and nearest, cannot satisfy *entirely and to the full.* At least I think not. But JESUS can. Perhaps you think I am preaching what may well suit those older than you; but that at present the Garden of Eden is rather for you than the Garden of Gethsemane; the tree of knowledge a tree to be desired, rather than the tree of the Cross. O believe me, I earnestly desire that you may be very happy, and may pass through boyhood, retaining all the freshness and innocency of childhood as far as may be; but I beg of you now that you are in the dawn of life, with so much even in the flowers, and shrubs, and insects around to love and rejoice in, with all GOD's good gifts around you, believe that herein, in really living a CHRIST-like life, lies your true happiness. Were we ready to see it, our best happiness is near, and requires no such straining after it as we often deem. Says a great modern writer, "To watch the corn grow, and the blossoms set; to draw hard breath over ploughshare or spade; to read, to think, to love, to hope, to pray,—these are the things that make men happy."

Therefore this term, and every term, keep one hour for CHRIST. Let your Sundays be to you especial holy days, wherein you may rest awhile from every-day bustle and work. Let your prayers by your bedside, morning and evening, be realities, bringing comfort and strength to you. At such times shut out all save CHRIST from your heart, and enter alone with Him into the Holy of Holies.

But while this is so, while such things are especially consecrated to GOD's service, at all times remember that you are in GOD's presence, and that His everlasting arms are ready to receive you, wherein you may lose yourselves and be safe.

> " White the lilies raise their heads,
>     Pierced with daylight through and through,
>   Red the roses bloom and glisten,
>     Smiling in the morning dew.
>
> " Will the darkness ever gather,
>     Wrapping all the earth in shade?
>   Will the night roll slowly on,
>     And the daylight sadly fade?
>
> " ' Enter thou into My garden,'
>     Whispers JESUS CHRIST to thee,
>   ' Watch with Me one hour apart,
>     In thy life's Gethsemane.
>
> " ' In the dawn of childhood's hour,
>     In life's noonday, *Watch with Me,*
>   Till the ebbing eventide
>     Land thee in *Eternity*.' " [1]

[1] By the author of these pages.

## XIV.

## TALENTS.

*" Occupy till I come."*—S. Luke xix. 13.

It was a bright summer's morning, and the gardener came forth to sow his seeds in the ground. And he looked around over his big garden, and saw that here and there were spots very well fitted for the growth of flowers, spots carefully sheltered from the rain and wind, yet open to the warmth of the sun ; other spots less favourable, yet where the soil was good and fertile; others again barren and hard, either wholly in the damp unwholesome shade, or exposed to the fierce glare of the sun at all hours of the day. And he sowed his seed and went his way. Now in this garden the seeds, under the sun's warm influence together with the kind rain, soon sprang up; and what had been but a short time ago but an unfruitful piece of land now shone brightly with flowers of many colours, some of greater, some of less beauty; and some of the fairer flowers of great size and uncommon beauty held themselves haughtily and disdained to look on those of lower degree. And ever and again the gardener came to watch the progress of his flowers, . . . and he looked somewhat anxiously at these proud ones which endeavoured to attract his attention, . . . and his eye rested rather with a smile of tenderness on some modest violets which lay back under a high wall, unobserved, save by the gardener's eye.

And again his eye would rest on, with very great love, and he would stoop tenderly down to, some poor weak plants struggling amid some bare and evil soil, where despite all their efforts to flower and please the gardener's eye they could only put forth a sorry flower.

So throughout the day these flowers grew ; and at even time the gardener came to gather a nosegay for himself. His face had something changed from tenderness to a more stern expression, and some of the flowers of greatest brilliancy on the instant of touching his hand withered up, and their beauty instantly was lost. And many of those weak nay almost ugly flowers, many of those which seemed least forward, when gathered into his hand, seemed all at once to throw out a richer brilliancy, and acquired a very great beauty ; and the gardener gathered his nosegay and left his garden.

This little allegory, boys, needs little explanation from me. JESUS CHRIST is the gardener ; this world is the garden ; we are the flowers growing in that garden. To each of us GOD has given a power to grow in this garden ; and He will assuredly come at eventide to reward us according to our growth. The words of the text say, " Occupy till I come." *How* can we occupy? Let us try to-night, and read the answer to these questions.

The word "*occupy*" in the Greek language means "busy yourselves," "take trouble," "do business." First, then, *When* ought we to begin to occupy? From our infancy? Yes, from earliest childhood, from our first breath. And when ought we to cease to occupy? With our *last* breath.

And *where* do we "*occupy?*" In our daily life, in our daily business, in our daily work, in our daily play.

> " The trivial round, the common task
>     Will furnish all we ought to ask—
>   Room to deny ourselves, a road
>     To bring us daily nearer GOD."

And *how* do we occupy? Well, on the answer to that question depends our condition when CHRIST comes to view our account.

What talents have each of us here to-night, and how are we wearing them? The earliest talent which we can turn to account is our *home*, our bringing-up—do not think this is a talent of little worth—not so ; it is a jewel very precious in the wearing, and very precious to look back upon in later life. Home! Does that word bring before you loving parents who have trained you in ways of holiness? A father, whose manly character, and wearing nobly the name of Christian and gentleman, taught you an example of a gentle, a noble, and a CHRIST-like life? A mother, to whom in your sorrows and trials you could turn and find comfort in her smiles, her kiss, her caress, her words?

Brothers and sisters, who as years rolled by, met by the old familiar fire-side, and breathed again words of love, and as they talked again of early happiness and childish joys, grew young again in memory? Yet are there those who can have no such memory, but only one of bitterness,

> Motherless, fatherless,
> Friendless and godless.

Many a child is born in misery, reared in the gutter, educated to vice from his cradle. Again, many a child has no bond of union, no sympathising love for its father and mother, brothers and sisters ; it is treated as one of a family, and its particular yearnings, hopes, fears, temptations, are left to shift for themselves. Then I ask you, Is not a happy home a talent, for which you will be assuredly responsible? Have the early lessons taught at a mother's knee, the strong words of a father or a brother, left their mark on your young life, to be dearly treasured and ofttimes brought out to be looked upon in the after time?

Secondly, take the talent of *Education*, such as you I hope obtain here. You have now the opportunity of gaining habits of work, habits of unselfishness only to be gained by numbers, habits of strength of mind and ability to say *no* to temptation. Here you are as much as may be shielded from evil, and those over you do try their best to plant the good seed of goodness, and truth, and purity,

and unselfishness, in you, that so you may grow up
Christian gentlemen, good soldiers of JESUS CHRIST.
And this education of body, mind, and spirit, is at
once awful and encouraging; it is awful, for whether you go to heaven or hell, whether you are for
ever joined or lost to those you love here, whether
you will do GOD's work or the devil's in this life,
largely depends on those older and supposed to be
wiser than you. Oh! if all those who have care
of the young could realize this. We laugh, as we
speak of a child being *spoilt*. Yes, indeed, do we
laugh if he be *spoilt* for all that is good, if he be a
curse to his home, living without GOD in this
world, and lost for ever in the world beyond? Do
we remember that as the tree falls so it will lie?
Do we not know well enough how the child imitates
the man, how our example far more than our talk
bears an influence that may "make or mar?"
Little acts of indulgence, because he is "such a
child," little permissions to do this, or not to do
this, because it seems so hard to refuse and so
pleasant to say, *Yes*—these are the beginnings of
an evil for which we are responsible to the child
and to GOD. O most awful thought! that in our
hands, in a parent's hands, in an elder friend's
hands, lies the weal or woe of many a young soul.
Yet there is encouragement also, for if the elder do
their duty to the younger, if those who have charge
of children (be they parents or masters) act not by
some imaginary theory of right or wrong, not by

what is always pleasant to our " darling" children,
if we are firm and gentle, stern to the sin, yet long-
suffering to the sinner; then the education of childhood is full of comfort and highly blessed.  It is
the setting forth well and betimes on the road to
GOD, a good start on the way of life, and a day's
march nearer home.  Remember, therefore, *this
talent*, and let us all look to it that we use it aright.

Or yet again, there is the talent of popularity, a
talent either very dangerous, or of all talents perhaps
the most to be desired; for by popularity we can
sway a multitude for good, and yet by popularity
we may in our fall drag down with us a multitude
into sin.  Be this popularity from our talents, our
attractive manner, our good nature, our general
power to be everywhere pleasant and liked, our
success in play, or our success in work; whoever has
it, and " thinketh he standeth, let him *take heed lest
he fall*."  In the larger world, the power to fascinate,
to gather around one a circle of admiring friends,
clever, witty, and cheerful, to be thereby welcome
everywhere, to be spoken of as successful, is no slight
and no uncommon ambition, nor is it to be condemned, so long as this power to move others serves
for a good purpose, and never stoops to mere self-
applause, to the common, yet GOD knows, natural desire to like and to be liked, or worse far to be misused
for evil purposes.  And in your little world of school-
life, who of you does not in his heart of hearts think
himself superior in this or that to his schoolfellows,

secretly looks down on them as his inferiors in one
pursuit or another, or if not so, *affects* a modesty
which he does not possess, in order to gain praise and
popularity ; or yet once more, if he says what he
thinks will please, and bring him praise, all the time
having no such real opinion ? Perhaps this power, or
at least desire to please, is now and then rather akin
to a virtue, yet, misuse it one iota, and it is a
spurious one, and viewed in its naked truth not far
from contemptible and odious.

And lastly; some of us possess in a far larger ·
sense than others, the *talent* of *religion*. I use the
word advisedly, for among the ancients, "religion"
meant the feeling of reverence for holy things.
And it is in itself, even if it proceed no further than
this, good to possess a Sunday of good thoughts
and impressions with which to surround our every-
day life ; it is good for us to treat holy things and
holy days with the respect they deserve ; it is good
and I believe it is natural, though more strongly
developed by far in one than another. So far
religion is emotion. One boy hears what moves
him well-nigh to tears. What he hears or sees, be
it what it may, touches some responsive chord, and
creates in him a fellow-feeling. Another boy hears
the very same, and to him the impression is nothing,
it touches him not, it passes and is gone. In things
of earth we feel this.

> " As for some dear familiar strain,
> Untired we ask and ask again,

> .  Ever in its melodious store,
>     Finding a spell unheard before."

Another listens, and to him it is but a tune, and
nothing more.   So in things spiritual, the instinct
of holy things is much stronger in one than another,
though I believe never wholly away from anyone born
into this world ; and surely the talent of seeing God
in all His works, of beholding Him in the forest, in
each insect, in the tiny leaf, in the roar of ocean,
and in the little brook prattling through the quiet
fields, the talent for reading aright the lesson,

> " The herbs we seek to heal our woe,
>     Familiar by our pathway grow,
>         Our common air is balm,"

of ever feeling " Thou God seest me" in every
thought and word, is a talent, if rare, yet of
unspeakable worth.

Such then are a few of the *talents* which you and
I must *occupy*.   They are not ours ; they are God's,
and we must return them to Him, bringing interest
with them.   Now, not a boy here to-night but has
*one, two, three, four, or more talents*.   Rear them,
cherish them, water them, that they may bring
forth abundantly, some sixty, some seventy, some
an hundredfold.   It is no merit of your own if you
are by nature more truthful, more generous, more
good-tempered than another, but it *is* a merit if you
increase those natural virtues day by day, and year
by year to perfection ; if you, yet possessing but a

faint portion of these virtues by nature, so "occupy" them that they become strong in you, and always at hand.

Therefore, my dear boys, "occupy," use your talents, do not abuse them, don't talk of them, don't exalt them into your own merits, but strive to make of them a ladder whereby you may ascend on high to the gate of Heaven. And "occupy" now, now, for the wise man occupies his to-day, for he knows not what his morrow may bring forth; so only will the Gardener rejoice to gather you into His hand; and He Himself has said, "Occupy till I come." And who of us can tell the day of His coming?

> "It may be in the evening,
>     When the work of day is done,
>   And you have time to sit in the twilight,
>     And watch the evening sun;
>   While you hear the village children
>     Passing along the street,
>   Among those thronging footsteps
>     May come the sound of My feet.
>   Let the door be on the latch
>       In your home,
>   For it may be through the gloaming
>       I will come."

Yes, JESUS of Nazareth is *ever* passing by among the flowers of His garden, and He sees us at hours when we little think of Him. Oh, are we so dull, so cold, that we cannot see Him? are we indeed *occupied*, but with selfish hopes, selfish fears, love of applause, thoughts of what others may think of us, so that we cannot *occupy* our hearts with CHRIST? Rather put Him first and foremost in your love, and so when He comes, you will be ready to offer Him of your best, be your talents and opportunities never so few, and your best never so poor. And if you say, "I have no talents, no opportunities, nothing wherewith to occupy till He come;" listen to the word of your dear LORD speaking to you in accents soft and low,

"My son, give Me thy heart."

## XV.

### DAVID.

"*Thou art the man.*"—2 Samuel xii. 7.
"*The Lord is my Shepherd.*"—Psalm xxiii. 1.

IT is a quiet valley, with tall flowers here and there shining brightly, where a shepherd boy sits watching his flock of sheep; listen to his song, "The LORD is my Shepherd, therefore can I lack nothing. He maketh me to lie down in green pastures: He leadeth me forth beside the still waters." That ruddy boy, with his fresh young complexion and bright eyes, singing his psalm of joy so gaily in the valley, is none other than David, the future king of Israel, the sweet psalmist whose

songs have gone forth into every land to be a blessing and a comfort to mankind at all time.   But
see ! along the slope come a bear and a lion, whose
aim is towards yonder flock, unsuspicious of their
danger.   Down they pounce on the sheep, and
seize upon one of the flock.   David shouts, and
careless of the odds, rushes upon them, and in the
strength of the LORD of Hosts, the young shepherd
boy kills both the lion and the bear.

Again, . . . years have rolled by : we are standing by the Valley of Elah.   No quiet valley this, but
one which resounds with the shouts of warriors, the
clanging of armour, and the cries of the fearful
host of Israel.   For none of the host can go
forth a champion to match the giant Goliath, who
towers in height far above all, and against whom
even King Saul, with all his daring and manliness,
dares nothing, but sits moodily in his tent.   But,
ha ! what is this?   A youth, little older than the
boy whom we just now saw, comes out in front of
all Israel with a sling and a few smooth stones,
against the giant with all his mail array.   Yes, and
he has slain the giant, and stands with his foot on
the body of him, who but a few moments ago defied the armies of the Living GOD.   What a proud
moment for David !   What an object of envy he
must *then* have been to many a heart both young
and old in that host !

Yet once again, . . . and alas ! that it should be
so, . . . and the words of part of my text ring in his

K

ears, " *Thou art the man.*"   Yes, " Thou art the man," who though King of Israel, feared far and wide for thy might, thy wisdom, thy royal majesty, hast taken the ewe lamb out of the bosom of the poor man and hast dressed it for thyself.   " Thou hast slain Uriah the Hittite with the sword, and hast taken his wife to be thy wife."   Can this be the playful boy who was tending his father's flock ? Can this guilty sinner, who has broken two of GOD's most holy laws, be the saviour of Israel, the man after GOD's own heart ?

And yet, . . lastly, . . and there is the sound of wailing, bitter and deep, and the rending of a heart well-nigh broken over the loss of a darling child, " O, my son Absalom ! my son, my son Absalom !  Would GOD I had died for thee, O Absalom, my son, my son !"   The son of his heart, his handsome impetuous son, had turned against his father, and after driving him into exile, and even well-nigh taking his life, at last met with a sad death at the hand of Joab in the forest.

And do you say, Why not have put rather only before us the life of the shepherd boy, the love for Jonathan, " passing the love of women ;" the king on his throne executing judgment and justice, alike beloved of his trusty soldiers and feared by his foes ; the aged monarch leaving his mighty kingdom to a son whose name should be famous, and who should maintain the house of David right worthily ?

And I answer, because we must see the man on

all sides. We all love David; we all admire his chivalry of spirit, his deep intensity of affection for his friend, his mercy to Saul in the wilderness, his confession of wrong, his noble bearing, his undaunted valour. David is a man who in his best and noblest moments is very great, very noble; and all his life through we feel sympathy for him, in his weaknesses and defects. He is not lifted up on a pedestal so high that we cannot reach up to his stature. His stature of grace and holiness is indeed high, but we can touch it, we can encompass it.

Now if these things are written for our example, upon whom the ends of the world are come; if these princes in Israel, and these saints of Old Testament lore are to us but human men and women with earthly weaknesses and sins clinging to their souls; let us see to-night what lesson we can learn from the life of David.

First, then, wholly clear your minds from the feeling that the men and women and children whose lives are set forth, whether in the Old or the New Testament, are not precisely in character, feeling, temptations, yearnings after the good, and falling many a time into the bad, alike to you and me. And this feature is very strongly to be felt in the case of David; the daily temptations, the daily fears, the daily prayers, the daily cares, the daily wants of David, are those which we feel every day, and every hour of our lives.

David is at once an example and a warning to us. He is our example; he possessed a large heart, ready to embrace the whole troubles of his country and his friends. He was a patriot, and desired that Israel should be the chief of nations, and should triumph over all foes. He had the tenderest love for the son of Saul, and seems to have possessed in a peculiar faculty the power of attracting people to himself. It is noble and something rare to see a heart which can appropriate to itself another's burden, and can by shifting half the load to itself ease another weary soul. It is rarer to see a heart which standing outside individual love can embrace a world outside, often in feeling and perception, inside only in that largest and most comprehensive circle, which forgets self in all. And highest of all, David felt an abiding sense of God's presence. The singer who cried, " Thou art about my path and about my bed, and spiest out all my ways," did not simply go to God in the hour of distress and sore need, he so lived as one encircled round day and night with the everlasting arms. He did not shut up his religion for Sundays, for special holydays, for the danger which calls on God by an inspiration in the word when all else fails; he ever remembered, " Thou God seest me." And the reason may be seen in the fact that he talked to God as a man talketh with his friend !

Have you ever watched a little, a very little child

in its smallest perplexity, in its least doubt, in its
dim misgivings as to right and wrong, how it goes
to its mother? In her presence there is safety,
away from her all is uncertainty. To her it prattles
out all its tiny joys, to her it whispers its tiny
sorrows; no one else, it feels, can care for it as its
" Mother," others may like and caress it for awhile,
but the truest, the longest love is for the Mother
alone.

Have you known the sympathy of a friend, such
a friend as was David to Jonathan, in whose presence you feel a repose, who in absence breathes
upon you a holy virtue, a restraint from evil, a
whisper to all that is pure and good, who when
you are yet a great way off in pain and anguish,
and even sin, runs to meet you, and refreshes you
with a great and blessed unity of heart and soul?

Well, then, such was GOD to David, from his
boyhood and all through his long and weary life,
he said to himself, "This GOD is my GOD, He shall
be my guide unto death." I beg you then, in this,
imitate David. My dear boys, carry GOD with you
everywhere, and to do so is impossible if you do
not live in Him. "His Will is our peace," wrote
the great poet of Italy,

"If thou wilt hear Me and wilt make thy choice,
    To follow where I lead,
As one who knoweth well his Shepherd's voice
    And loves the sheltered mead,
Then in fair peace shall all thy heart rejoice.

Then thou shalt find it in the meadow wide,
   Where whitest flocks are fed,
In pastures green, with it shalt thou abide,
   By living waters led,
With it from noon-day heat in deepest shadows hide."

David put GOD first, and so long he had *peace*, peace in his state and peace in himself. He did not wait till he had had his "fling" of life, till the best of his days were over, and in the evening of life thought it well to make peace with an angry GOD. He found GOD in childhood.

"When he was following the ewes, great with young ones, GOD took him," and in all his failings and sins he turned to GOD as to his FATHER, exceeding wroth with the sin, yet his FATHER and his GOD. Yes, learn, in his very faults to imitate David. He sinned grievously, yet in the hour of his deepest guilt, he poured out the offering of a broken and a contrite heart, the murderer and the adulterer, the proud numberer of the people; he broke GOD'S commandments by sins of the deepest dye; yet for all this, though his sins were as scarlet, GOD washed them in His boundless sea of mercy and compassion, for he was heartily and truly sorry for his sin, and set himself steadfastly to seek after GOD.

Lastly, from David take warning: in his *greatness* David was weak. We pray in our beautiful Litany, "In all time of our tribulation, in all time of our *wealth*, in the hour of death and in the day of judgment, good LORD, deliver us." "In all time of our *wealth*, ay, most truly do we thus pray, for at such time are we apt to forget GOD.

> " When the world around is smiling,
>   In the time of wealth and ease,
> Earthly joys our hearts beguiling,
>   In the day of health and peace,
>     By Thy mercy
>   O deliver us, good LORD."

In our *sorrows* we remember GOD, in our joys we are apt to forget Him, or put Him by to a more convenient season. A great writer, Addison, called for his nephew, a young man of wild and vicious life, on his death bed to witness " how a Christian can die." Rather let us look to it, " how a Christian can live."

And oh, be sure of this, and if you do not understand it now, you will most assuredly, hereafter. It had been a thousandfold happier for David if he had never sinned. The death of his child by Bathsheba, the revolt of his dearest Absalom, the turning away of the hearts of his people, the deaths of those countless numbers for his one sin of numbering the people, think you these brought no grey hairs, no deep cut wrinkles, no furrowing of the brow, no heart-sore to the son of Jesse? He is the happiest boy or man, she is the happiest girl or woman, who have not soiled their robes in sin and therefore in sorrow, and whose guardian angels do not abandon them for awhile in shame and grief, who have no page of their lives which is dark and blotted with tears for sin. O believe me, confession (as was David's) for sin is noble and good. Humble persistence and a steady resolve to amend, is the sign of a melted heart eager to atone for the past; but is not the snowdrop most clear, because most innocent and most pure? Never think a knowledge of evil to be grand and manly. It is neither grand nor manly. Never regard the curbing of self, the strong restraint of evil passion, as hard and irksome. You hear people say, "We long to see the world." If you mean GOD's world, GOD's flowers, and trees, and sea, and mountains; if you mean GOD's world of intellect whereby man can fashion noble books, noble pictures, noble deeds; if you mean GOD's world of noble speech, noble society, noble love—then long, if you will, and it will be well with you, but if you mean the world without GOD, the world that runs after excitement that never satisfies, the world that offers pleasures that bring no true happiness, the world that worships self as its God, then long not for this, or it will be ill with you. Even in this life, it is so desperately hard to retrace lost ground. The greatest French novelist of the day has described a man who was a convict, and who having escaped from prison roams about in France, constantly pursued by the police, and ever in fear of being taken. He has set before himself a better life, a giving up of the old bad ways of stealing and murder—He in his disguise grows rich and honoured in a country town in France, and is made Mayor. All at once he is discovered, and has to fly, he lives disguised in Paris, and there does many acts of charity, and all he can for the poor. Once more the police find him out, and to his last hours he lives in dread of being once again thrown into prison.

Jean Valjean, the convict, found it very hard to whitewash his sins over and to acquire peace even with the world around him. So it is with all of us, good is it for us, if along the narrow way that leadeth to life, we only here and there wander off in quest of flowers that prove briars, to pick sweet berries that are rotten and foul. But how unspeakably better if we can (as far as lies in us by GOD's help) keep along the road all the way with our eyes fixed on the Cross and Him Who hangs there, looking *forward* only, neither to right nor left. It is true, with David to say, "Blessed is he whose unrighteousness is forgiven." It is more true with David to say, "Most blessed is he in whose spirit there is *no guile.*"

----

## XVI.

## PRAYER.

*" I will arise, and go to my father. . . . And he arose, and went."*—S. Luke xv. 18, 20.

" I CANNOT find words," says a great writer and thinker of to-day, "to express the intense pleasure

I have always in finding myself at the foot of the
old tower of Calais Church. . . . It stands with no
complaint about its past youth, in blanched mas-
siveness, gathering human souls together under it.
The sound of its bells for prayer still rolling through
its rents : and the grey peak of it seen far across
the sea, principal of the three (peaks) that rise
above the waste of surfy sand and hillocked shore
—the lighthouse for life, and the belfry for labour,
and this for patience and praise." May we not say
of this with Jacob, "This is none other but the
house of GOD, and this is the gate of Heaven?"
Or, again, come to the porch of the little village
church with its old embattled tower, its windows
half hidden by ivy, its small troop of worshippers
in simple attire, entering the house of GOD as "a
haven where they would be" for a brief hour, away
from the plough and the labour of sheep and oxen.
See the family of the village gathered round to
pray and praise, far away from the dust and bustle
of the town world, asking for blessings on their
quiet homes, their parson, themselves, and all they
love,—ay, and in this hour of service to GOD shar-
ing in prayer with the larger life beyond sound of
the village bells, and breathing for a little while in
the hymn of worship mounting from each village
spire, each town church, each lofty cathedral in the
land, to the ear of our one FATHER.

Or yet once more, turn from the gay streets of
Paris into yonder quiet church on a weekday, when

the world without is busy in its holiday, and chancel
and aisle are a cool retreat, where we may enjoy a
little space apart and think of GOD. It is getting
dusk, and the labour of to-day is well-nigh over.
See the market woman or the labourer enter for a
moment, and laying down the basket or the load
of labour beg GOD's blessing, and go forth in the
strength of that prayer better men and women, for
at least a little space.

Or, lastly, stand in GOD's great cathedral of
Nature at eventide, when the last flush of rosy
day has ebbed, and night comes over the sky;
out come the stars one by one "in their courses;"
and out of the womb of the dark tabernacle of
cloud issues the moon, wrapping hill and dale in
her silvery veil, and casting a broad path of liquid
beauty on the ocean. Arcturus and his sons come
forth with Orion and the sweet influence of the
Pleiades. "This hath GOD done, and we perceive
that it is His work."

To sum up then these four scenes of GOD's
presence : GOD is in the lone, grey-headed pile of
Calais Church; in the quiet village kirk; in the
house of prayer in Paris streets, in the still evening
spread everywhere. If we then arise, and go to
our FATHER, He is not far from any one of us;
nay, He is in our midst; and yet from the very
nearness, we ofttimes miss Him. We look for
Him enthroned in a cloud of glory : we pass Him
by in the lilies of the field and the grass that we

tread on : we stand gazing into Heaven in an inspired rapture and have no eyes for the hill of
misery and sorrow *at our feet*.   And yet this knowledge that GOD is everywhere is not enough to
satisfy my hunger ; my jealous soul cries out for a
GOD for me.   I must enter into my closet, and
shut to my door with a GOD to Whom I can pour
out my every thought, and hope, and prayer, be it
never so feeble, never so small.   The little child
smiles upon all, is willing to be caressed by all,
accepts toys from this one, and a kiss from that
one, yet it is for his father's look of approval, for
his mother's smile of tenderness that he turns in
real concern, seeking a place to hide his little trials
and troubles.   The prodigal son is hugged to every
breast, and is welcome everywhere ; but his heart
*will* back to his father's house, to the old home,
to the only love in the world worth having : " I will
arise, and go to my father."

O the largeness and exact beauty of GOD's great
and most excellent law !  O my GOD, give us grace
every one to worship Thee aright one with another
in the great congregation where with all men in
the communion of saints on earth, we bless and
thank Thee for a life laden with mercy, as also to
whisper to Thee our inmost heart, the very marrow
of all our life in this world and the next.

First, to-night I would say a very few words on
GOD as our FATHER meet to be worshipped openly,
and in temples made with hands ; and, secondly,

on GOD as our FATHER to be sought for in private prayer in the sanctuary of our own hearts.

First, then, as to public prayer. It is very old in habit, it stirs up enthusiasm and mutual help, it inspires others towards worship. It is *very old in habit.* The Greek beheld GOD everywhere. GOD was to him in each cave, each flower, each fountain. A child of nature himself, he saw GOD in all His works. His church was nature, his daily service the spectacle of GOD's good gifts, seen in the sea, the earth, the changeless hills, the flowers. As a child the Greek cried aloud in pain, but went not of course to his God for medicine in his sickness; he saw his God everywhere, yet grasped him nowhere. He was not the peculiar God of Pericles, or of Nicias, or any one Greek; he was the God of the nation. Thus by enlarging his God he dwarfed him; yet, that due honour might be paid to the unknown God, gorgeous temples adorned with the most costly gifts were reared, where the especial presence of the God might be felt, and his or her statue might serve for an object of admiration. If we turn to the pages of the Bible, we early find Noah building an altar to the LORD: and the patriarch Jacob found in the stone at Luz the holy presence of GOD and His Angels. GOD bestowed upon His ark a more immediate and local glory in the eyes of the children of Israel, and Solomon "built Him a house." The loss of their first lovely temple was an intense grief, repaired however by the constructing of a second only inferior to the first in beauty. In the days of JESUS CHRIST on earth synagogues, or places of meeting together, were common, and CHRIST Himself both entered into them and partook of their service. At the first, after our LORD's departure from earth, from alarm of persecution, the early Christians held services apart in fear and trembling, but as time went on, and in the person of Constantine a Christian Emperor for the first time sat upon the throne, splendid churches began to be erected far and wide. Relics more or less old remain to us in our old English Abbeys of Crowland, Beverley, Tintern, and later, Westminster and elsewhere,—relics of a time when men gave of their best for GOD, and when all that art and skill of workmanship and abundance of wealth could do, reared noble memorials which live even as far as to us of this generation.

Secondly ; public worship stirs up *enthusiasm* and *mutual help*. Enthusiasm exists in crowds, not in one single man, and the burst of feeling on all sides creates a flood of joy bubbling up untold in the heart. We hear music of passing sweetness ebbing and flowing in some old minster ; we see a lovely lake, fringed with trees thick with leaves of various tints. We listen to the eloquence of a speaker, carrying us out of ourselves into a higher and stronger atmosphere,—do we not feel, "O that he or she were now with us ! O if only every one could see or hear this, what an effect it would have—a nation on their knees at prayer! Is this impossible to realise? Perhaps for this country England has shown few nobler sights, few more wonderful to the foreign mind than a nation eager for news of the fate of the Prince of Wales but a few years ago as he hung betwixt life and death. And I have never seen a grander sight than the Prince restored to health, his queen mother, his wife, accompanied by a nation's blessings and thankfulness, passing on to the great cathedral of S. Paul, there to bow the knee in gratitude to the GOD Who gave a son back to his wife and his mother, a Prince to the people who had prayed for him. Public prayer is most helpful against a selfish spirit. Were we only to pray in secret we might be in danger of asking GOD's blessing only on ourselves and those we love. But this were not well. Better in the words of our Litany, " That it may please Thee to have mercy on all men ; We beseech Thee to hear us, good LORD." And surely the sight of numbers known or unknown to us met to render thanks for the great benefits they have received at GOD's hands, to set forth His most worthy praise, to hear His most holy Word, and to ask those things that are requisite and necessary as well for the body as the soul—surely this sight of the House of GOD sending forth as it were a great cry that will pierce even to the throne of GOD Himself, cannot but stir us one and all to

greater seeking after GOD, more fervent charity one
with another, a keener desire to understand the
things of GOD.

Thirdly; public spirit puts before all the opportunity, the means, and the spectacle of arising and
going to their FATHER. None can say, "I have
an excuse, I have no house where I can meet
GOD; I have no ladder whereby I can climb up to
Heaven." There is GOD alike at the foot and the
top of the ladder set up in well-nigh every village,
and in all towns in England. There, Sunday after
Sunday, if not every day, you can hear the words
of that oldest and best of books—GOD's holy
Word; you can join in joyous psalms and hymns
that rise up as incense to the throne of GOD; you
can hear the preacher sowing what good seeds he
can in a few brief minutes, after he has watched
the thorn and the thistle for six days growing up
and choking the word of life. No, those who will
not enter and drink of the water of life have but
themselves to thank. Yet even to an indifferent
heart the sound of holy bells calling to prayer
and praise cannot be wholly as nothing. And it
takes time and an effort to the child of GOD to
forget the day of rest, the Church of GOD, and the
holy influence of our good old English Service.

And then, lastly, What can I say of the use of
*private prayer?*

They only know who have best tried and felt its
sustaining power. The Book of Common Prayer

is indeed noble, ay, and marvellously beautiful,—
yet it is common, and we cannot bear that the world
should always see our inmost heart. If GOD is our
dearest and best Friend, our FATHER, our all, we must
put all else for a while outside this holy of holies.
Our longing and deepest love are not for the eye
of others to pry into ; they belong to GOD, and He
only can wholly sympathise with us, wholly lead
us to rest all on Him, in that loving silent confidence which argues perfect love.

Thus do we pray *for ourselves*. Others around
us do much for us, bear long with us, think they
understand us,—but Thou, O GOD, alone knowest
because Thou alone seest the heart.

> " While many sympathising hearts
>     For my deliverance care,
>   Thou in Thy wiser, stronger love
>     Art teaching me to bear."

Never, my dear boys, give up this habit of praying *for yourselves* night and morning. For he who
prays aright cannot well but live aright. If you
can tell GOD all in prayer, twice daily, and feel
that nothing remains behind that you have not
laid before Him, then your conscience will be clear,
and your heart free of offence.

And why should it not be? Why, but because
sin, your evil desires and acts, create a something
between ourselves and *our Father*. Time was when
we told Him all; time was when we ran to Him

L

in our little sorrows and trials; time was when we confessed our wrong, and begging for forgiveness rose from our knees at one with GOD. Ah, but a something has arisen between us and GOD which was not there before,—is it we who are changed, or is it GOD?

And yet again, let us pray not only for ourselves but for others. In the old legend when King Arthur lay dying, and his knight, Sir Bedivere, the last of the band who once sat at the Round Table, had cast his king's noble sword, Excalibur, into the Mere, there came ladies three and bare the dying king hence in a barge, leaving the bold Sir Bedivere alone, the last of the band of knights on the shore. And what comfort can Arthur leave him? Seems it to you but small, or of all comforts one of the best?

" Pray for my soul. More things are wrought by prayer
Than this world dreams of. Wherefore let thy voice
Rise like a fountain for me night and day.
For what are men better than sheep or goats
That nourish a blind life within the brain,
If, knowing GOD, they lift not hands of prayer,
Both for themselves, and those that call them friend?
For so the whole round world is every way
Bound by gold chains about the feet of GOD."

O most unspeakable is this blessing, this high privilege, that though no man may redeem his brother, we can send up strong intercession for him. "O GOD, guide him to see the right way; make him more and more to walk in the way that leads to Thee; make him stronger, better, holier; and this I beg for JESUS CHRIST'S sake." Does the father or the mother never so pray for the prodigal son who is now a great way off? Does not such prayer plead for those who are leading lives away from GOD, as also for all whom we love, and who have not set their affections on heavenly things? Therefore, while we ever pray, "GOD be merciful to me a sinner," let us not forget the larger prayer of our great Master CHRIST to His and our FATHER, "FATHER, I will that they also whom Thou hast given Me be with Me where I am."

Prayer is the key of heaven—prayer alike *public and private*. With it we can open the door that leadeth to the perfect Communion of Saints. Do you fear to enter? Fear not. For if we fear to go to our FATHER, to whom else shall we go? He knoweth His own sheep, and He will recognise each one of you. Thus it will be only exchanging a far-off cry from our knees, be it in church or at our bedside, for speaking face to face with Him; and though here earthly friends may forget, and earthly love grow cold, His perfect love will encompass you about, and know you for His own.

> " Can a woman's tender care
> Cease towards the child she bare?

> Yes, she may forgetful be,
> Yet will I remember thee."

O believe me, prayer is stronger than death, stronger than life, your best resource, your most perfect time. Therefore if you would pray, as we all once learned to pray, in simple trust at a father's or a mother's knee, if you would live, and we can so live, (if we could only see it,) the life of peace, which ¡without prayer can never be, ask GOD to-night to give you this *gift* of prayer, this *spirit* of prayer, and be sure, quite sure, you will be better boys this week, better boys this term, better men in after years, better fitted for that heaven where prayer is lost in praise. Do you think that prodigal son could see before him how his return should be? Could he scarce hope, he so long away from his father's home, so long reckless of the only true happiness? Come with him to your FATHER; come, and your cup shall overflow with blessing; come, ere yet you wander from your FATHER's home, and your prayers now so faint and fearful, shall be answered if only you cry, "Not my will, but Thine be done."

> "I said, 'The darkness shall content my soul.'
>    GOD said, 'Let there be light.'
> I said, 'The night shall see me reach my goal.'
>    Instead came dawning bright.
> I bared my head to meet the smiter's stroke,
>    There came sweet dropping oil;
> I waited trembling, but the voice that spoke
>    Said gently, 'Cease thy toil.'

I looked for evil, stern of face and pale,
  Came good, too fair to tell;
I leaned on GOD when other joys did fail,
  He gave me these as well."

Yes truly, for "so He giveth *His beloved*
peace."

---

## XVII.

## HEAVEN ON EARTH.

"*In the beginning God created the heaven and the earth.*"—
Gen. i. I.

EVERYTHING new, everything perfect; such was
the condition of heaven and earth in their infancy,
fashioned by the hand of the great Maker. Not
one blemish, not one defect, not one excess were
there; no, "GOD saw everything that He had
made, and behold it was *very good.*"

We in our finite mind cannot grasp the infinite.
There is nothing infinite save GOD and GOD'S
handiwork; therefore, every work of man, however
grand, sublime, and towering near to Heaven,
cannot be perfect and entire. For one moment
let us endeavour feebly to conceive of this creation
of heaven and earth. Out of a bleared and in-
distinct mass of objects, hopelessly carried hither
and thither without object, energy, or system; out
of a chaos of dark mist brooding over a world

restlessly tossing to and fro in space, out of nothing, came forth the very perfect and only beauty which never tires, the order which never changes, the heaven and the earth.   We, in this life even, if we will look around us, can see yet glimpses more or less perfect of this creation of GOD; and the more fully, and the more with enjoyment of things lovely and ennobling, the more we know of the mind of GOD, so much the more we shake off the impurities of taste, sense, and feeling, which withstand the power of exactly appreciating GOD in His works, nay, even in the works without GOD.

Yes, thus arose the world from the hands of its Maker; and how has man changed GOD's world? Man began by murder, "Cain rose up against Abel his brother, and slew him."   And yet in the Bible history it seemed not so very long before we read, "So GOD created man in His own image, in the image of GOD created He him."   Then a little further on in the Bible page, "And GOD saw that the wickedness of man was great in the earth, and that every imagination of the thoughts of his heart was only evil continually."

With the deluge, and the saving of Noah and his family, a new season began in the world's history. It might have been thought, that a warning so awful as a world drowned, all save eight souls, might have served to keep the new world of man good and holy, but experience teaches that often no warning of the past, no future heaven and hell, are powerful enough to turn the sinner from his way, and only create *remorse*, not godly *repentance*. And so mankind growing bigger and bigger in number grew also in sin. From the days of wicked Sodom and Gomorrha until to-day, men have grown old in sin. I will not say the world has grown old in sin, for GOD's world has not so erred, but only those in it who so pollute it from its beautiful nature into an evil world. Let us take one example, a daily one, for examples of our every-day life must come most home to us. We go out into the fields at this season of the year fresh from the labour of producing the fruits of the earth, among the quiet lanes encircled by the changing tints of autumn spread on every tree; we feel life glow within us in the warmth of a summer's day, or in the silent hush of a light winter frost, when the trees are overlaid with silver. Do we any the less refrain from unkind words or foolish talk of other's failings? do we any the less hold back from anger and words of discontent? I fear not often; for GOD's beautiful world is not for us to enjoy, it only is good in our eyes as a means to gratify us, not as a silent teacher, hearing our foolish and wrong talk, seeing our evil deeds. I beg you think this no fancy, but see in all around you, however apparently wonted and small and ugly, a token of GOD, a memory of the Creator. "All Thy works praise Thee, O LORD," "GOD saw *everything* that He had made, and behold it was very good."

Or yet once more, we turn over our newspapers. What a scene of life, of a new world, lies in these few sheets, man's pleasure, man's business, man's glory, man's deeds! Ay, but where is the Maker's pleasure, the Maker's business, the Maker's glory, the Maker's deeds?

Not in the foul list of crime that daily recalls the spirit of Cain, or of other breakers of GOD's holy commandments; not in the spilling blood that glory may dwell in our tents, and that a new tract of country may be ours; not in the successful bargain which makes men roll in wealth at the expense of the poor fools who being less sharp or more scrupulous are brought to ruin; not in the gilded slavery which turns man into a machine only capable of making the point of a pin or the head of a nail to an exquisite perfection. Is this a list which shows that we of the nineteenth century are wiser, nobler, better than our fathers were, and that our world of to-day is to be compared to the world of which we read in our text, " In the beginning GOD created the heaven and the earth?"

We, I take it, are gone sadly from our perfect state of creation; and why? Because we will not see GOD's created gift. " GOD created the heaven and the earth;" we make the earth our *all*, and will not see the heaven. We lose heaven in earth, and yet, could we but see it, could we but lift the veil which is before our eyes, we should see the Angels of GOD around us, and a heaven on earth.

Do you say, how can these things be? let me very briefly tell you to-night.

Now there is a most beautiful text which says, " whatsoever things are true, whatsoever things are honest, whatsoever things are just, whatsoever things are pure, whatsoever things are of good report ; if there be any virtue, and if there be any praise, *think on these things.*" And yet once more, speaking of the *Kingdom of God*, S. John in the Book of Revelation, declares, " There shall in no wise enter into it anything that defileth, neither whatsoever worketh abomination, or maketh a lie." Now, boys, *here* is the Kingdom of Heaven set up on earth ; we must not only regard GOD as in Heaven, and ourselves upon earth ; we must see GOD and hear Him in our daily life, our daily struggles, our daily sorrows.

What stands between earth and heaven ? Sin— this only. And how can we create our heaven here ? By bringing GOD to us—by seeing GOD in all the unspeakable blessings around us—by seeing JESUS CHRIST in the sympathies and fellowship of earth—by receiving within us the HOLY GHOST to comfort—so shall we be exalted from earth to that heaven, whither CHRIST has gone before.

O GOD the FATHER, teach us to see Thee aright in Thy beautiful world, in Thy mercies of life, and health, and hourly blessings. O JESUS CHRIST, teach us more of Thyself, and give us more of Thy SPIRIT, that bearing one another's burdens we may so fulfil Thy law. O blessed Comforter, fill our souls with Thyself, and give us that inward peace to abide with us ever, which the world cannot give.

First, then, *do* see the happiness of heaven in the lovely world around you. Herein, in the intense beauty of flowers and shrubs, trees and fruit, in the sky, and in the sea, in all that we see, lies a heaven of happiness.

> " The golden sunshine, vernal air,
> Sweet flowers and fruit, Thy love declare—
> When harvests ripen, Thou art there !
> Who givest all.

> " For peaceful homes and healthful days,
> For all the blessings earth displays,
> We owe Thee thankfulness and praise,
> Who givest all."

O could we not think of our FATHER as so far off, but as very near every one of us in His every gift, we should not regard Him only as " Our FATHER Which art in heaven," but also as the giver of " our daily bread"—the giver of all good things.

And secondly, we must, if we discern this "earthly paradise" with true eyes, at once live a life of inner holiness and peace ourselves, as also lead others with us into this communion with CHRIST. And this, not by a multitude of professions, not by much talk, but by example and action. We must first possess this *life of peace* within ourselves—O do not think you are too young to have it ; possess it now, and be possessed by it. It is not to be got by going out of daily life; take it with you in your daily life here and at home. Rear up this sabbath of peace and content in your week-day life.

Wrangling, evil thoughts, angry words and deeds, selfishness, pride, these cannot enter in, for heaven knows not such. Have this happiness in yourselves first, and then you cannot but give it to others. Your life here or at home may be quiet, repeating itself daily, yet it is a life of peace. There are those who in this world "carry music in their heart, with whom the melodies abide of the everlasting chime." Oh, having found peace to yourself, find it for others. Think of what it would be to say with truth at last—not only "I have fought a good fight," but also, "I have brought my brother to CHRIST, I have put happiness into the sick heart, I have poured balm upon the weary soul—I have brought the pilgrim of hope to the covert from the storm, safe home at last." O untold blessing! O best and most perfect heaven of happiness to have fed another with the manna of divine love and sympathy, tenderly bearing another's burden, planting sweet flowers of mercy and hope in the weary path of life. Try and help, not hinder others; don't see all the ill you can; don't think all the ill you can; don't do all the ill you can. Will it be so small a thing, say at the end of term, to have made those around you bright, happy, yes, and better for your example, or even your word? O you will really, most really, feel

an inward happiness of which you know nothing
unless you have tried.

> "To comfort and to bless,
>   To find a balm for woe—
> To tend the lone and fatherless,
>   Is Angel's work below.
>
> "The captive to release,
>   To GOD the lost to bring,
> To teach the way of life and peace,
>   It is a CHRIST-like thing."

Thirdly and lastly. Suffer GOD'S HOLY SPIRIT
to make your heart His resting-place. There is a
hymn which says,

> "Ah when wilt Thou always
> Make our hearts Thy home?
> We must wait for heaven:
> Then the day will come."

But I would rather say to you—No, you need
not "wait for heaven." "*Now* is the acceptable
time. *Now* is the day of salvation." Do you not
find, time after time, that *earth* is all to you? Do
you not feel at times (if you would be truly honest)
that you could do *without* prayer, without church,
without service to your FATHER, without an ascension of hope and feeling, but that you could ill do
without games, amusement, and pleasures? Do
you not feel that it is so *easy* to yield to the wiles
of Satan, so hard to smite him down? Well, have
the HOLY SPIRIT in you, pray for the HOLY SPIRIT.
Your happiness will be no less, your games and

pleasures will be no less; but you will with them all have found the one thing needful. You will in having GOD'S HOLY SPIRIT ever abiding with you have an oracle sure and unfailing to whom you may go and find an answer in time of doubt and need. You will regard your duties as something sacred, not things to take up and lay down at will, but as a trust committed to you by GOD.

It was a little child, walking in a great plain, where under his feet was hot sand, and where the water of the stream looked foul and muddy, and where only nettles and brambles grew on a few bare patches of grass. And on he walked, day by day; and he thought to himself, "This is a long and weary way, and there ever seem before me the same sand and water, and nettles, and brambles." And he stooped down to drink of that water, and behold it was marvellously sweet! And he took of the sand in his hand, and it became bright gold; and at his touch the nettles and the brambles blossomed forth into beautiful flowers.

So will you, if you grasp aright the sense that earth and life contain blessings in the wearing, that here on every side is a heaven, a tabernacle meet for GOD, in daily struggles and efforts after better things, come at length to see GOD'S created heaven here. Likely enough, to you, your duties seem the same; your work, your play, and your routine seem very ordinary; but look on them and on your schoolfellows with new eyes, seeing good for evil, and sweet for bitter, and you will understand those words that bring "GOD near to every one of us."

"And I saw a new heaven and a new earth, and I heard a great voice saying, Behold, the tabernacle of GOD is with men, and He will dwell with them, and they shall be His people; and GOD Himself shall be with them, and be their GOD." Unto which eternal heaven may GOD bring us every one for JESUS CHRIST's sake.    Amen.

---

## XVIII.

### SILENCE.

*" There was silence in heaven, about the space of half an hour."*—Revelation viii. 1.

I THOUGHT it was the time of summer; and the trees were clothed with leaves, and the gardens were heavily laden with rich fruit and flowers, brightly the birds sang, rejoicing in the warmth of the sun shining forth over hill and dale.   Nothing worked save the bee, active in his chase for honey. And far away amid the copses and green fields wound the river as a silver streak gaily dancing in the sunlight.   All was warmth, all was silence.

And yet, once more it was night, and in the still hours the moon arose over the sea; and as I sat in the stern of the vessel, and saw the long white line of foam trailing far behind, there was nought around but sea, sea and sky peopled with very many lights : the sea was asleep, and rested in the still embrace of the heaven enfolding the waters in blessed silence. Then methought I entered the city where arose the self-same moon, and the self-same stars that shed their light on the calm sea.

Gaslit streets, excited crowds, misery, noise, un-ease, words of anger, discontent, strife, these were on every side. Rest there was none—The hush of silence was not here, no not from early dawn till day yet break again, all was unrest, sorrow, strug-gling, impatience . . . . This was *man's* world—yonder (that we first spake of) was GOD's world.

And if there be silence on *earth*, what of this silence in *Heaven* of which our text speaks ! We can dare just for a moment to peep past the veil of the unseen, and see GOD as He is, arrayed in Glory with Angels and the great Communion of saints gathered in Heaven.

There is GOD Himself, He Whom no eye hath ever seen, the *Almighty*, the *Invisible*, the GOD who was from time unborn, and shall be till time shall be no more, being swallowed up in eternity. The LORD GOD Who made man out of the dust of the earth ; the GOD of Abraham, Isaac and Jacob, the great I AM of the children of Israel, the GOD of Adam, the GOD of you and me, the GOD to Whom in all ages men have cried even though they knew Him not, Whose ears have heard the cry of this,

and may be of other worlds, since first He put man
in the Garden of Eden—(can we pause for a brief
moment to conceive of the cries of anguish, the
beseeching prayers for grace and pardon, the prayers
of the great host of men arising up as clouds of
incense, the whisper of the sinner, "GOD be merciful to me?")—the GOD Whose eyes are too pure
to behold vanity; Whose eyes in their large gaze
have looked ever since the fall of the first man on the
fall of millions, on the births and deaths of men
and women born to be a blessing or a curse, on the
waste, the evil, the sorrow of a world grown weary
in sin—yes, (and GOD be thanked) on the strivings
after good, the outward and visible signs of Cathedral and Church and places meet for GOD's Service,
on the inward and spiritual signs of fervent charity,
holy lives and holy deaths—yes, this is GOD. And
at His right hand is the Lamb of GOD slain for us,
JESUS CHRIST, "the same yesterday, to-day, and
for ever;" and there is the Comforter, He Whose
breath pours holiness into our hearts. Around stand
saints made perfect in glory, and an innumerable
multitude of those who have fought a good fight
on earth, and now are at rest in that home "where
the wicked cease from troubling, and the weary are
at rest."

Yes, even here in this heaven where all conspires
to raise hymns of praise in one shout of triumph,
there was SILENCE. Why was there silence? Because the seventh seal was opened, and at that

hour came up to Heaven the prayers of those on earth.

O supreme moment, when thus a door is opened in Heaven by the merits of JESUS CHRIST, whereby the speech of those on earth yet fighting, struggling, hoping, faintly and afar off, may climb even into the presence of GOD! O sweet communion wherein the saints above whom we lost awhile draw near through these prayers to us, and watch eagerly for them to be put forth before GOD, knowing that herein is our strength and sure confidence, our present help in trouble—GOD make our prayers worthy of such ascension, through JESUS CHRIST our LORD.

And if thus silence in Heaven is perfect, can silence on earth never be perfect? When is silence good and right? Often.

First. It is a sign of strength. CHRIST was silent before the High Priest, and the crowd of chief priests and Pharisees. And He answered Pilate never a word, so that the Roman governor marvelled. Knowing His cause was right, and that no power of words could convince those who were present that His was the only true cause, CHRIST forbore to speak, " He held His peace." Look at ourselves. How often, knowing ourselves really to be in the wrong, do we cover our fault with a multitude of words, with ready excuses, which rise to our lips. He who is guilty need not talk loudly, for words but increase his guilt; he who is innocent need not talk loudly, for words do not increase

M

his innocence. If so be that at times, here or at home, now or in later life, you are misunderstood; if so be that you have tried to make for a better and holier life; if so be that you have prayed and striven to upset this besetting sin, and yet those around you know not, and find fault again, and rebuke you for slipping once more—bear it in silence—believe this is best—believe that in silence is the better, ay, the best part. Learn from JESUS CHRIST that in *silence* ofttimes lies your true strength. He was oppressed, and He was afflicted, yet He opened not His mouth; "He is brought as a lamb to the slaughter, and as a sheep before his shearers is dumb, so He openeth not His mouth."

Secondly. Silence shuts the door to the possible lie. Does not every one here to-night know well that we in our hearts like our actions not only to be good, but also to seem good to others? we don't like ourselves to be thought worse of than we think we deserve; we like to be liked by others. Then, if on a sudden we fall into a fault, and suspicion rests on us, we are sorely tempted, are we not? to give a reason—perhaps a possible reason—for our actions. "I should have been quite diligent, only I had not time; I should not have said that untruth, only I had no time to think; I should not have taken all for myself, and left none for nobody else, only I really didn't think what I was doing." Are these excuses *to* ourselves or *for* ourselves hourly or daily?

And this feeling arises largely from *vanity*. We cannot bear to be lowered in the eyes of others, as we foolishly fancy we shall be, if they know that we have given way to this weakness, or left undone a supposed or real duty. But remember, "Thou GOD seest us," and before that gaze into our heart can we dare to make excuses which fail even to satisfy ourselves! Therefore, avoid excuses as dangerous, and likely to lead us into greater evil.

Thirdly. Silence is good, for "it suffereth long, and is kind." It can say no evil, it can utter no abuse, it can give no cruel wound. Turn to the words of *one day*, and see what they are, to us, to others, to GOD; if "kind words can never die," so also evil words, harsh words, biting words, words of ill temper, die hard.

*Words as to themselves.* Do we not speak better of ourselves than we deserve? Do we not so talk often that others may fancy us to be better than we really are? Do we not speak of this or that as especially hard to *us*, as if forsooth we endured all hardship and vexation and misery, and besides there were none.

*Words as to others.* Of all things what is more sunny, more joyful, than a spirit of happiness, which sows happiness all around, and bears good fruit in kind words and kind actions? and as this is sunshine, so most cloudy and repulsive in the sight of GOD and man is the spirit which is for ever finding fault, ever seeing wrong motives, ever disliking *what is* in *what might have been*, causing a sullen gloom to its owner's spirit and to all around. We would fain be thought clever and witty, and to have said something to create a laugh. Is it at another's expense? Is it to turn some one else into ridicule? Is it to say something true indeed, but uncalled for, and better unsaid? GOD knows we one and all require "to keep the door of our lips," lest we offend our souls and those of others.

*Words as to God.* Do we profess a religion we feel not? I need not to such an audience enlarge on this, for the young are *well and rightly* wont to speak not openly too much of religion, of GOD, of things lovely and pure, but look to it that your silence breed deeds of brotherly love one to another. "Let your good deeds (in silence) shine before men!"

And lastly. There is sympathy in silence, a sympathy beyond words, too deep for talk. That happiness is the most *intense*, that sorrow is the most *intense*, which *feels*. Yes, there are times when words are too poor to express thought, and silence is supreme rest. We pass from out the outside clatter, and the walks of common-place talk, into a sacred shrine where alone perfect communion is possible. In that shrine lies our treasure : in that sanctuary is all our heart : there is perfect trust ; there is sacred obedience.

It was a beautiful garden, and the sun shone

gaily on the flowers of many colours : and as the first breath of early morning passed over the garden, breathing a sweet balm into every petal and leaf, a smile broke over each flower rejoicing in the sunny gaze of Heaven : and the tall white lilies raised their slender heads proudly towards the blue sky, and said among themselves, "We are sure of the prize which the Lord of the garden gives this evening for the *best* flowers ; surely we are best, for we are nearest Heaven." And near by, the carnations rivalled them in beauty, saying, " We are not born to blush unseen ; for we too are admired by all, and the Lord of the garden takes more pleasure in us than in aught else." So the morning wore on into afternoon, and at eventide the Gardener came. And He paused not, but stooped down, where a rose modestly lay back out of sight in a quiet recess of the garden, and He gathered it and put it near His heart. And the breeze of evening came up and said, "Where is the rose?" and the birds came forth to sing their evening hymn, and they said, "Where is the rose?" and the stars came out one by one in the sky and whispered, "Where is the rose?" and they said, "The Gardener took it to His heart, and hath taken it Home."

So will it be with us, believe me, when our evening comes. They will be gathered nearest the Great Gardener's heart, not those who have said, " LORD, LORD," professing much and doing nothing ; not those who have thought of themselves and cared

little about wounding the feelings of others by harsh
and unkind speech, not those who have looked
ever at Heaven, and forgotten the things of earth,
of daily life at their side : but they rather who
have *in silence* possessed their own souls with perfect charity and tenderness stretching thence to
the souls of others, whom their own *silent* lives
teach by a divine spell, preaching a gospel of love,
felt, read, understood, unspoken.

" Silent in the winter soil
    Lies the winter grain ;
  Silent grows the sower's toil
    'Mid the dreary rain :
  Will the corn be gathered ever
    With its sea of golden foam ?
  Will the reapers sit together
    In the summer harvest home ?
  *Silent* work we, good seed sowing
    Where the thistle thickest lies ;
  *Silent* reapers—daily growing
    In the grace which GOD supplies.

" Silent is the sleep of GOD's unending rest,
  Silent is the call of them that love Him best ;
        Silent teachers,
        Silent preachers,
  GOD take us all to His all-tender Breast !
  Silent is the sleep of GOD's eternal rest,
  Silent the Heaven of His Holy Breast,
        Pillowed ever,
        Nought can sever
  Us from JESUS, if we only love Him best."[1]

[1] By the author of these pages.

## XIX.

## EDUCATION.

*"My Father's business."*—S. Luke ii. 49.

IT has been the great object of mankind ever since the world began, first to find their "FATHER," secondly, when found, to do His "business." By that I mean, all men have so desired, who have not been merely finding out their own pleasure on earth and doing "self's business" with much activity.

The world took a very long time finding out its FATHER. The *first* man knew Him, for he owed Him all, but he did not do His "business:" for he ate of the tree of which his FATHER had said to him, "Thou shalt not eat." The *second* Adam, JESUS CHRIST, knew Him, for He came forth from the FATHER, and all His life through He said His "meat" was to do His FATHER's will; and with His last breath on the Cross of Calvary He cried, "FATHER, into Thy hands I commend My spirit."

Come aside this evening a little while and see these three who are speaking together. For I thought in my dream that I beheld, and lo there was one in the dress of a Greek, one in the garb of to-day, and a little child. And I know not why, but there rose to my lips the words of a beautiful line in the Word of God, " And a little child shall lead them." A little child may put to shame the learning of the Greek groping blindly after an " Unknown God," and the self-conceit of the nineteenth century talker on education who says, " It shall not be an *offence* if teachers shall enforce the duties of kindness, &c., by illustrations drawn from the Bible."

Yes, indeed, it has been reserved for our century, a century very wise in invention and manifold research, to find out this invention, that *God's* word is unequal to *man's* word—that kindness and virtue are well-pleasing to man, and not first and far more well-pleasing to God—not rather that, if we would increase in the wisdom and stature of a Christian life, finding favour not only with man but also with God, we must learn what God's saints in all ages did, how they behaved under the trials and temptations which are the lot of all time and of all people, how the child Joseph grew to be strong in God's grace, how the child Samuel waxed mighty in the strength which God supplies, how the Child Jesus lived and died—I say, herein is our best, our highest *education*, could we but see it, and educate ourselves from it.

And methought this Greek, beautiful of form and endowed with every grace, was speaking of his education, and he said, " I am the child of the gods, but yet how can I educate myself from them ?

For the stories of the gods say that they do vile acts, yea, that they exceed in wickedness all that men can do or can conceive of in their hearts. Wherefore it seems that a god is only a man of infinite power for good or evil, working in himself (or in herself) that which best pleases them. So I have no guide, for I know not pleasure save in the things of earth around me. I rejoice in the blue sky, the green fields, the purple vine, the fountain, and the sea. I endeavour to excel in strength of limb, that I may gain the laurel leaf of the great games, and may smite down my foes, achieving for myself mighty renown. I desire to be skilled in art and sculpture, and in the 'music' of the soul, for these things are great and exalt me to nobler aims. I know not whence I came or whither I am going. I desire to be *perfect*, but how to be so, I know not better than this."

This is the Greek's cry—this is the Greek's education—how should it be otherwise? And I turned to the teacher of the nineteenth century, who desired that GOD and GOD's Word should be left out of teaching, lest GOD in His Word should offend the taste of the reader or hearer. And he said, " I learnt many legends at my mother's knee. I learnt that GOD made the world in six days; that a paradise arose for man, wherein he might be perfectly happy, so only he ate not of the tree of knowledge of good and evil; that a flood destroyed all the world save Noah and his family;

that the Son of God took man's flesh and died for man.   But these and many like stories I now see are good neither for children nor for grown men; for they are idle fables.   We of to-day are wiser than our fathers, for they walked by faith, believing that the Word of God cannot lie : but we have received a new oracle, even the oracle of our new wisdom.   And we wish our children to learn the rules of the ten commandments, that they steal not from us, nor tell lies to us, nor swear vainly, nor do acts of violence and impurity, and so forth : but we will not further teach them that these commandments are written by God's finger, for to tell them the Author of these ten rules would be a hindrance to them.   For this is like as though there lived a great King, who made laws for his citizens, which they one and all confessed to be good and followed them, and said that those who broke them erred, but they themselves dared not so much as whisper the name of the great King, for He is not admirable—(only are His laws admirable)—and besides, the citizens of their own unaided wit might have contrived laws equally good."

And he having spoken, the little child said to them both, "And Jesus called a little child unto Him, and set him in the midst of them, and said : Verily, verily, I say unto you, Except ye be converted and become as little children, ye shall not enter into the kingdom of heaven."   But neither

the Greek nor his neighbour would receive this
word, for they thought within themselves that their
mighty intellects cannot stoop to the condition of
a little child ; and that reason is to be preferred to
faith. Wherefore they prefer to stand outside the
Kingdom of GOD.

But, my dear boys, "ye have not so learned
CHRIST." You at your Baptism were signed with
the sign of the Cross, that hereafter you should
fight manfully against the world, the flesh, and the
devil ; you were brought into CHRIST's great fold ;
you have been brought up in an education drawn
from GOD's most holy word; you have been taught to
call GOD " Our FATHER," and your aim is set before
you, to do " His business."

What a blessed, holy, yet awful sight is the young
child. A soul to be saved or lost ! one who shall
do GOD's work or the devil's ; one, whose "business"
will either be to the praise and glory of GOD, or the
slavery of Satan. Reading a life the other day, I
read of the feeling towards children possessed by
that brave soldier, Sir W. Napier. " His tenderness
was never so marked as when he was looking at, or
talking with little children. Towards these little
creatures he had an eager way of stretching out his
hands as if to touch them, but with a hesitation
arising from the evident dread of handling them too
roughly."

And in this wide subject of education, so wide,
so immense, that we are ever devising new schemes

and new improvements, there seem certain great
points for us to lay hold of, which are ofttimes
neglected strangely even by those who profess they
love their children, and would have them grow up
good men and women.

First, then, what means of education does GOD
provide? He endows us with a body, a mind, a
soul; He puts us in the midst of His own created
world, and His own created creatures. And He
wills us to be *happy*. Can we doubt this? Do
we ask, why then does He send us temptation and
sorrow? Because they are good for us, because they
lead us to rest on Him, because they draw us to
see a heaven on earth. And how much sorrow is
our own fault! Sorrow for our own sins, sorrow for
the sins of others, sorrow that we are imperfect and
cannot see GOD as we ought. But to a little child
all is Eden; he wanders about in the garden, and
sees everything "very good;" to him everything
that he sees, or feels, or tastes, is new, and conveys
a first pleasure. And in his GOD he finds the most
perfect sympathy, alike in sorrow and joy; for a
child requires this sympathy. He delights to show
his new toy, his new present, his collection, to
prattle his little tales; he yearns to meet with
sympathy over the broken toy, the lost present, the
bigger griefs of parting from home and dear friends.
Ah! sadly do they misunderstand children, who
always say, "How silly to make so much of a toy,
a doll, a plaything!" Yes, but to the child, whose

world may be his nursery, or at best a very small area, the joy and sorrow are as great relatively as to you grieving over your bigger sorrow, rejoicing over your bigger joys. Therefore the prayer of the little child, "O GOD, give me a new doll," has nothing ridiculous in it. It is the cry of a little one believing that He cares for the loss, and alone can help the sore trouble.

Like Adam in the garden, so the little child sees GOD in his garden of life. He has but one lesson to learn as Adam had,—obedience. If his father or mother bid him, he must obey, and this will not be hard to him if he from his earliest childhood learns this. He believes that they know best, and it does not occur to him that their command can be foolish; he has faith in them; he cannot conceive that they would harm him or lead him into wrong. But suffer me to insist on obedience *and* happiness,—not one *without* the other, but one *with* the other.

Think for yourselves. If you perfectly trust any one as perfectly knowing the better thing for you, would you rather follow your sweet will and choose the worse? You say, No; but this is what disobedience is, this is what Adam did. Unless a child learns this lesson, that he must submit to authority, that "spoiling" means ruin,—he has missed part, I must say all, of the real happiness. This is education, that a child from his earliest days obey. GOD did not explain to Adam where fore he might not eat of the tree; He gave him the commandment, and the punishment consequent on disobedience.

Thus the child having learnt to give up his pleasure, finds a new pleasure in doing little acts for others. And with his perfect obedience will grow a perfect love. "Perfect love casteth out fear." Adam only feared, having sinned. And if the child feels that punishment is the only thing to fear, not rather the having displeased GOD as well as those over him, he has an education quite incomplete. For there is, I do firmly believe, in every child an instinct which would lead him to do the good, to desire heaven, to please GOD. But ofttimes the child, growing into the boy, loses this instinct, because he misses that education which should "prevent rather than cure." It is so desperately hard for the grown man to wash away his sins and to find GOD; it is so far easier, so far better, so far happier, from our earliest days never ·to have lost Him. Why should it not be so? Why do some of you who sit before me feel that you are not what you once were, that strange thoughts creep into your prayers, that you have, alas! sadly fallen from the vows made for you at baptism, that you do not seek this first, "to do your FATHER's business?"

There are *sign-posts* to show you the way. If Baptism was the first one on the road to GOD, there are many before Confirmation. There are

Sundays.   What are your Sundays to you? what
have they been since first you went to GOD's
house, and even before that?   They surely err
and break one of GOD's holy commandments who
teach children to make no difference between the
"day of rest," and the days of labour.   Never lose
the belief that Sunday is a good day to you, a day
of doing GOD real service in His house, a day of
thinking seriously, "Am I a better boy than I
was? am I trampling out that fault which I know
so often attacks me? am I trying, feebly though it
be, to do my FATHER's business?"   Let your Sunday be no day of irksome gloom, but a happy (not
a merry) day, not given to play, but possessed by
a sense that this seventh day has other surround-
ings and another atmosphere than the six days of
the week.

Another sign-post is *prayer*.   As with your Sundays, so I earnestly beg you never to lose the
habit of prayer.   The soul that has no speech the
whole year through with its GOD, neither in His
service nor in prayer, is dead, and puts forth no
good fruit.   Therefore pray.   Has GOD ceased to
be your FATHER? has He forgotten to be gracious?
has He not showered mercies upon you?   Then
follow prayer, for indeed it is a lovely and a pleasant thing.

And many other sign-posts there are,—such as
reading GOD's holy Word, hymns, the lives of
saints of GOD, home affections, and so forth.   All

which ought to further education in its best and truest sense.

Is such your education? For such a child having learnt that in obedience is happiness, that all happiness is innocent and good for use, that in perfect love he can ask GOD his FATHER for daily bread and daily blessings, will step by step grow more like that perfect Child JESUS CHRIST.

> " For He is our childhood's pattern,—
>    Day by day like us He grew :
> He was little, weak, and helpless,
>    Tears and smiles like us He knew :
> And He feeleth for our sadness,
> And He shareth in our gladness.''

Go and do thou likewise.

---

## XX.

## UNSELFISHNESS.

*" And they lifted up their voice, and wept again: and Orpah kissed her mother-in-law; but Ruth clave unto her."*—Ruth i. 14.

THE story of Ruth is one which perhaps some of us here to-night do not know very much about. There is nothing of stirring interest in this little book of four chapters. There are no battles, no fighting as between David and Goliath, no hairbreadth escape of David flying from Saul, no

Daniel cast into a den of lions, no, it is the story, the simple story of a life.

Ruth was a woman of Moab, and was on her husband's death left with her mother-in-law Naomi, and her sister-in-law Orpah. Naomi's home was at Bethlehem-Judah, and she resolved to return thither. Orpah and Ruth proposed to go with her to her native land, but Naomi begged them not to do so, begging them to remain in the land of Moab amid their old home and friends. Orpah kissed her mother-in-law, and stayed, "but Ruth clave unto her." Here we have in five simple words the history of Ruth. She doubtless had much to pull her back to her own native land, associations, memories, friends, and it was a wrench to depart for an unknown land, for an unknown people, for an unknown God. But we see the hand of GOD in this, constraining her to choose the better part. Few nobler or more touching words are to be found in the whole Bible than these spoken to Naomi, " Intreat me not to leave thee, or to return from following after thee : for whither thou goest I will go, and where thou lodgest I will lodge ; thy people shall be my people, and thy GOD my GOD ; where thou diest I will die, and there will I be buried ; the LORD do so to me, and more also, if aught but death part thee and me." So they went until they came to Bethlehem, and here in the City of Bread, they found bread enough and to spare.

N

I have no time to-night to pursue the story, how
Ruth went a-gleaning in the field of Boaz, the
kinsman of Naomi; how she found favour in the
eyes of Boaz; how Naomi in her old age found in
Ruth a love "better to her than seven sons;" how
as the wife of Boaz she became through David's
line the ancestress of JESUS CHRIST, and thus in her
seed, the families of the earth were blessed.

The story dwells not on these unspeakable blessings, nor does it enlarge on the crowning mercy of
GOD in giving to the descendants of Ruth that
blessing of all blessings, which the mothers of
Israel desired and yearned for with untold longing, to have the Messiah born of their race.

These blessings Ruth could not see, no, nor
imagine, as she went forth with Naomi from her
home to the land of Judah. But GOD seeth not
as man seeth, and having surrendered herself up in
simple trust, and put aside self, that so Naomi
might obtain all comfort, she received in every
way a most high and perfect happiness.

And what lesson may we learn from her and her
simple story? First, notice her utter loss of self.
*She lost herself in Naomi, and so in God.* I have
often spoken to you of the beauty of unselfishness,
and the curse both to itself and to others of a soul
filled with self. Bear with me yet once more to-
night, if for a few minutes I bring before you this rare
and most lovely gift. Remember, Ruth knew nothing of the blessings soon to be poured upon her.

She only saw a road winding up hill all the way,
yet she saw it with glad eyes, for along it were
strewn the flowers of self-sacrifice and unselfish
love. Oh, is it not very hard to forget self?
And yet after all, why is it so very hard? Well,
we hear so much of self on all sides; we are told
that the victory is for the strong, and that the
weaker must go to the wall. We see success ap-
plauded, and high in favour. Our every-day life
seems all self, save and excepting a few brief
minutes given weekly to GOD's service; wherein
also we are very deeply concerned how *we* sing—
how *we* praise—how *we* pray.

Boys, this is not well. To-morrow morning will
come; the week-day routine succeeds to the greater
rest of to-day; self again comes to the fore. Of
selfishness itself there are different classes. There
is a *petty* selfishness—a mean selfishness, which
all would deny with contempt that they possessed,
—a selfishness as to what we eat and drink and
wherewithal we shall be clothed. This is the lowest
selfishness, and near akin to the beast who cares
only for his meat and drink. Hence comes the
selfishness of indulgence—letting ourselves do just·
what we like—such is indifference to the pain we
cause to animals because forsooth we derive pleasure. And because " selfishness" (as " lying" and
" stealing") is an ugly word, we find an excuse for
ourselves in the thought that the animal or insect
does not feel, and that we are doing a benefit

either to science or our own health.   And so indulgence to children is among the worst forms of
selfishness—for while the best happiness is perhaps
only seen in children, and while all that is bright
and  beautiful and  loving is for children, and in
children, still is it a sin in GOD's sight to save ourselves annoyance, or the charge of unkindness, or
(worse) trouble—regarding children as "sure to
come right," and thinking that "one must make
allowances for those who are so young."   Yet this
selfishness will only recoil on the head of its author,
for a child who has had his education of *self* only
developed, will be little likely to have regard to the
feelings of others, when *himself grown to riper age.*
So the selfish child grows up to be a  selfish man,
and dies uncared for and unbeloved.   If we reflect
for a moment, on this lower motive, what boy
does not care far more for another, who gives up
little pleasures, who is always bright and sunny,
who speaks no words of discontent and fretfulness,
than for another however clever and strong, who
never gives way and only seizes everything for
himself?   And surely GOD, Who sees the heart,
must expect some love for Himself.   Love must
beget love.   Assuredly the love of GOD, Who gives
us all things freely to enjoy, Who strews so many
blessings everywhere in our path, Who has given
us happy homes and dear friends to love and care
for us; nay more, Who long ago sent down His
only SON JESUS CHRIST to die for us and  make us

heirs of Heaven; assuredly, the Love of GOD is not a thing for us to cast aside, or coldly to think nothing of.

Secondly; in unselfishness such as Ruth's, there must be *self-denial.* These two virtues go hand in hand. There was once a man in very ancient times, so the story goes, to whom the gods ordained to die, unless his father, mother, or wife should die for him. And this man was so selfish that he begged his father and mother to die for him and to save him alive. But they would not. Then his wife, whose name was Alcestis, of her own accord came forward and said that she would willingly die for his sake, that so he might for a little while again see the sun come down over the hilltops and day break over the earth, and still evening grow slowly into night. And as the last evening of her young life came on, and she sat with her hand in his watching the lengthening shadows creep over the purple hills, where grew the ruddy grape in many vineyards, and the silent air was only broken by the bleating of sheep or the tread of the tired husbandman going home from his labour, as she saw each insect and bird, each beast, each man, welcome night, she sat on and thought, "There shall be no morrow for me. The glorious summer day will be shed over the beautiful earth, and all that the gods have made will rejoice in the bright warmth, and man and beast will arise refreshed for another day. But for me there is no morrow—kiss me, O my husband, and think well of me when I am gone." "Greater love hath no man than this, that a man lay down his life for his friends." This was the self-denial of the heathen woman Alcestis.

Or yet again. It was the time of the wild Revolution in France, and the city of Paris was full of crime and blood, for the mob had arisen and cried, "Death to all!" And one lay there in his prison cell, doomed to die on the morrow by the cruel guillotine. And as he sat alone thinking of his dear wife suffering in anguish of spirit for him, as there floated over him memories of dearest affection and tenderness,—never, ah, never again to be recalled; and as he so waited for the morrow of death, when he, as hundreds more, should be led out amid the jeers of the multitude to a base death,—the door opened, and there entered a young man whom the prisoner in days gone by cared little for, and had deemed merely idle and good for nothing. And this young man having made him insensible to what was happening had him conveyed out of his dreadful cell, and put himself in his place. And the sun arose on a saved life, far away from the scene of bloodshed, in England,—and a lost life far away also from the scene of bloodshed, even in that country which is very far off. That young man, Sidney Carton, had given all he had; and forgetting self lost a life, and saved a life.

Once more, "Greater love hath no man than this, that a man lay down his life for his friends."

Yes, and lastly, if such are examples of a very noble unselfish denial of self—What shall we say of the self-denial of our great example, of JESUS CHRIST? To His side come not the lovers of self, the lovers of pleasure only, the lovers of satisfying their appetites and lusts. No.

> "Art thou weary, art thou languid,
> Art thou sore distrest?
> Come to Me, saith One, and coming,
> Be at rest."

At rest! yes, in that Bosom, in those Arms there is rest for the weary pilgrim, for the penitent sinner, for all who honestly press forward to the mark of the high calling which is in CHRIST JESUS. Does self-denial seem very hard to you? Does unselfishness seem so very far off? You are not called upon to give up innocent happiness, a crown of loving-kindness in home and friends, and all that earth has most beautiful. But now, to-night, to-morrow, this week, this month, for the rest of this year *resolve* that you will by GOD's help be more like this woman whose life we have read of, more ready to give up, more happy in others' happiness, more sympathising in their troubles. It will be a hard task at first, and few, very few will own that they are selfish, so subtlely does self attack us one and all. O, I beg you, do not let these poor words of mine fall fruitlessly to-night, let them bring forth

fruit in a more serious endeavour to deny yourself
in your every-day life . . . . a stronger endeavour
by GOD's help (without which we can do nothing,)
to be more unselfish in thought, words, and act.
Do not go and forget this lesson to-morrow, or even
to-night, but ask GOD at your bedside to help you
to watch yourself in this matter; ask Him to guide
you in all your ways, that so like Ruth you may
put yourself into His Hands, holding fast to Him
in trusting confidence.   So will you, like her, come
to Bethlehem, even to that peace of happy *good
doing* which is our best happiness here and hereafter,
to that most perfect well-being which I pray GOD
to grant to each one of us.   But ever recollect—

" No cross, no crown."

J. MASTERS and Co., Printers, Albion Buildings, Bartholomew Close.

# A LIST

# Theological and Devotional Works

# J. MASTERS AND CO.,

## 78, NEW BOND STREET, LONDON.

# A LIST OF
# THEOLOGICAL AND DEVOTIONAL WORKS

### PUBLISHED BY

# J. MASTERS AND CO.

---

## THE REV. J. M. NEALE, D.D.

**A COMMENTARY ON THE PSALMS,** from Primitive and Mediæval Writers; and from the various Office Books and Hymns of the Roman, Mozarabic, Ambrosian, Gallican, Greek, Coptic, Armenian, and Syriac Rites. By the late Rev. J. M. NEALE, D.D., and the Rev. R. F. LITTLEDALE, LL.D. Four Vols. Post 8vo., cloth, £2. 2s.
Vol. 1. *Third edition.* Psalm I. to Psalm XXXVIII., with Three Dissertations. 10s. 6d.
Vol. 2. *Second edition.* Psalm XXXIX. to Psalm LXXX. 10s. 6d.
Vol. 3. *Second edition.* Psalm LXXXI. to Psalm CXVIII. 10s. 6d.
Vol. 4. Psalm CXIX. to CL. With Index of twelve thousand Scripture References. 10s. 6d.

**SERMONS PREACHED IN SACKVILLE COLLEGE CHAPEL.** Four Vols., Crown 8vo.
Vol. 1. Advent to Whitsun Day. Second Edition. 7s. 6d.
Vol. 2. Trinity and Saints' Days. Second Edition. 7s. 6d.
Vol. 3. Lent and Passiontide. Second Edition. 7s. 6d.
Vol. 4. The Minor Festivals of the Church. Third Edition. 6s.

\*\*\* The Author's popular "READINGS FOR THE AGED," Four Vols., third Edition, are included in this series.

**SERMONS PREACHED IN A RELIGIOUS HOUSE.** Two Vols., Fcap. 8vo., 10s.

**SERMONS PREACHED IN A RELIGIOUS HOUSE.** Second Series. Two Vols., Fcap., 8vo. 10s.

**HISTORY OF THE HOLY EASTERN CHURCH.**—General Introduction. Two Vols., £2.

**THE HISTORY OF THE PATRIARCHATE OF ALEXANDRIA.** Two Vols., 24s.

**SEATONIAN POEMS.** Fcap. 8vo., 3s. 6d.

**MEDIÆVAL HYMNS, SEQUENCES, AND OTHER POEMS,** translated by the Rev. J. M. NEALE. Second Edition. 2s.

**HYMNS FOR THE SICK:** for the hours, days of the week, &c. 6d., cloth, 1s.

**HYMNS FOR CHILDREN.** First, Second, and Third Series. 3d. each. Complete in cloth, 1s.

# THE REV. T. T. CARTER, M.A.,

### Rector of Clewer; Hon. Canon of Christ Church, Oxford.

**THE DOCTRINE OF THE PRIESTHOOD IN THE CHURCH OF ENGLAND.** Third Edition. 4s.

**THE DOCTRINE OF CONFESSION IN THE CHURCH OF ENGLAND.** Second Edition. Post 8vo., 6s.

**SERMONS.** Third Edition. 8vo., 9s.

**SPIRITUAL INSTRUCTIONS ON THE HOLY EUCHARIST.** Crown 8vo. Fourth Edition. 3s. 6d.

**SPIRITUAL INSTRUCTIONS ON THE DIVINE REVELATIONS.** Crown 8vo. 4s.

**LENT LECTURES.** 8vo., cloth, 8s.
  1. The Imitation of our LORD. Fifth Edition. 2s. 6d.
  2. The Passion and Temptation of our LORD. Second Edition. 3s.
  3. The Life of Sacrifice. Second Edition. 2s. 6d.
  4. The Life of Penitence. Second Edition. 2s. 6d.

**FAMILY PRAYERS.** Fourth Edition. Cloth, 1s.

**THE DOCTRINE OF THE HOLY EUCHARIST,** drawn from the Holy Scriptures and the Records of the Church of England. Third Edition. Fcap. 8vo., 9d.

**PARISH SERMONS ON CHURCH QUESTIONS.** By the Rev. T. T. CARTER, M.A., Rector of Clewer, and Hon. Canon of Christ Church, Oxford. Fcap. 8vo. 1s.

### EDITED BY THE REV. T. T. CARTER.

**A BOOK OF PRIVATE PRAYER** for Morning, Mid-day, Night and other times, with Rules for those who would live to GOD amid the business of daily life. Tenth Edition, limp cloth, 1s.; cloth, red edges, 1s. 3d.; roan, 1s. 6d.; calf, 3s. 6d.

**LITANIES AND OTHER DEVOTIONS.** 1s. 6d.

**MEMORIALS FOR USE IN A RELIGIOUS HOUSE.** Second Edition. 6d.

**NIGHT OFFICES FOR THE HOLY WEEK.** 8vo., 2s. 6d.

**THE FOOTPRINTS OF THE LORD ON THE KING'S HIGHWAY OF THE CROSS.** Devotional Aids for Holy Week. Fcap. 8vo., cloth, 1s.

**FOOTSTEPS OF THE HOLY CHILD,** being Readings on the Incarnation. Part I., 1s. Part II., 3s. 6d. In 1 vol. 4s. 6d. cloth.

**MANUAL OF DEVOTION FOR SISTERS OF MERCY.** In Eight Parts, wrapper; or, Two Vols., cloth, 10s.

**SHORT OFFICE OF THE HOLY GHOST.** 1s.

# THE RIGHT REV. A. P. FORBES, D.C.L.,
### Late Bishop of Brechin.

**ARE YOU BEING CONVERTED?** Sermons on Serious Subjects. Third Edition. Fcap. 8vo., 2s.

4

[*J. Masters & Co.,*

**SERMONS ON THE GRACE OF GOD,** and other Cognate Subjects. 3s. 6d.

**A COMMENTARY ON THE LITANY.** Fcap. 8vo., cloth, 3s. 6d.

**A COMMENTARY ON THE TE DEUM,** from ancient sources. Royal 32mo., cloth, 1s.

**A COMMENTARY ON THE CANTICLES USED IN THE PRAYER BOOK.** Royal 32mo., cloth, 1s.

**A COMMENTARY ON THE SEVEN PENITENTIAL PSALMS,** from ancient sources. Royal 32mo., cloth, 1s.

**THEOLOGICAL DEFENCE** for the Bishop of Brechin on a Presentment by the Rev. W. Henderson and others, on certain points concerning the doctrine of the Holy Eucharist. 8vo., 6s.

**A PRIMARY CHARGE DELIVERED TO THE CLERGY OF HIS DIOCESE.** Third edition. 1s.

EDITED BY THE BISHOP OF BRECHIN.

**MEDITATIONS ON THE SUFFERING LIFE OF OUR LORD.** Translated from Pinart. Fifth Edition. 5s.; calf antique, 10s.

**NOURISHMENT OF THE CHRISTIAN SOUL.** Translated from Pinart. Fourth Edition. 5s.; calf antique, 10s.

**MEMORIALE VITÆ SACERDOTALIS;** or, Solemn Warnings of the Great Shepherd, JESUS CHRIST, to the Clergy of His Holy Church. Translated from the Latin. Second Edition. Fcap. 8vo., 3s. 6d.

**THE MIRROR OF YOUNG CHRISTIANS.** Translated from the French. With Engravings, 2s. 6d. Cheap Edition, 1s.


# THE RIGHT REV. J. R. WOODFORD, D.D.,
### Lord Bishop of Ely.

**SERMONS,** preached in various Churches of Bristol. Second Edition. 7s. 6d.

**OCCASIONAL SERMONS.** Vol. I., 7s. 6d. Vol. II., 7s. 6d.

**ORDINATION SERMONS,** preached in the Dioceses of Oxford and Winchester, 1960—1872. 8vo., 6s. 6d.


# THE RIGHT REV. R. MILMAN, D.D.,
### Late Bishop of Calcutta.

**THE LOVE OF THE ATONEMENT;** a Devotional Exposition of the 53rd chapter of Isaiah. Fourth Edition. Fcap. 8vo., cloth, 3s. 6d.

**CONVALESCENCE.** Thoughts for those who are recovering from Sickness. Fcap. 8vo., 1s.

**THE VOICES OF HARVEST.** 8d.; cloth, 1s.

**THE WAY THROUGH THE DESERT;** or, The Caravan. 6d.; 1s. cloth.

**MEDITATIONS ON CONFIRMATION.** 3d.

# THEOLOGICAL, &c.

**ACTS OF THE APOSTLES, The.** An Exposition of the leading Events recorded in that Book. Cloth, 1s.

**ADAMS, Rev. R.**—A Commentary on the Prayer Book, for the use of overworked Pastors and Teachers in the Church and School. Fcp. 8vo. 4s.

**ARDEN, Rev. G.**—Manual of Catechetical Instruction. 2s.

**BAGOT, Mrs. C. W.**—Selections from the Letters of S. Francis de Sales. Translated from the French. Revised by a Priest of the English Church. Fourth edition. Fcap. 8vo., cloth, 1s. 6d.

**BLACKMORE, Rev. R. W.**
The Doctrine of the Russian Church, &c. Translated from the Sclavonic-Russian by the Rev. R. W. Blackmore. 8vo., 4s.
Harmony of Anglican Doctrines with those of the Catholic and Apostolic Church of the East. 8vo., 3s.
History of the Church of Russia, by A. N. Mouravieff. Translated by the Rev. R. W. Blackmore. 8vo., 10s. 6d.

**BOOK OF GENESIS, The.** An Exposition of the Leading Events recorded in it. Fcap. 8vo., cloth, 1s.

**BOOK OF CHURCH HISTORY,** founded on the Rev. W. Palmer's "Ecclesiastical History." Fifth edition. 18mo., 1s.

**BROWNE, C.**—A Lecture on Symbolism and its connection with Church Art, Architecture, &c. Third edition, with 42 Illustrations, and Appendix on the Symbolism of the Ecclesiastical Vestments. 1s. 6d.

**BROWN, Rev. R. C. L.**—The Life of Peace. Fcap. 8vo., 2s. 6d.

**CATECHISM OF THEOLOGY.** 18mo., cloth, 1s. 6d.; wrapper, 1s.

**CHAMBERLAIN, Rev. T.**—The Epistle to the Romans. With Short Notes chiefly Critical and Doctrinal. Fcap. 8vo., cloth, 2s.

**CHAPTERS ON THE TE DEUM.** By the Author of "Earth's Many Voices." 16mo., cloth, 2s.

**CHRIST IN THE LAW;** or, the Gospel Foreshadowed in the Pentateuch. Compiled from various sources. By a Priest of the Church of England. Third Edition. Fcap. 8vo., 3s. 6d.

**CHRIST IN THE PROPHETS:** Joshua, Judges, Samuel, Kings. Fcap. 8vo., 4s. 6d.

**CHRISTIAN SERVANT** (The) taught from the Catechism her Faith and Practice. By the Author of the "Servants' Hall." Edited by the Rev. Sir W. H. Cope, Bart. Fcap. 8vo., cloth. (Pub. 7s.) *Reduced to 3s.*

**CHURCH DOCTRINES PROVED BY THE BIBLE.** Fcap. 8vo., 1s.

**COMPANION TO THE SUNDAY SERVICES** of the Church of England. 2s. 6d.

**DAILY EVENTS OF HOLY WEEK.** Written in Plain Words. Fcap. 8vo., 6d.; cloth, 1s.

**EASY LESSONS FOR THE YOUNGER CHILDREN IN SUNDAY SCHOOLS.** By the Author of "Conversations with Cousin Rachel." 4d.
Questions, for the Use of the Teacher. 6d.

**EASY CATECHISM OF THE OLD TESTAMENT HISTORY,** with the dates of the principal events. Third edition. 18mo., 3d.

**ECCLESIOLOGY,** Hand-Book of English. Companion for Church Tourists. Cloth, 2s.

**EUCHARISTIC MONTH;** being short Daily Preparation and Thanksgiving for the Holy Communion. Cloth, 1s.

[J. Masters & Co.,

**FASTS AND FESTIVALS OF THE CHURCH**, in a conversational form. 1s. 8d.

**FORD, Rev. J.**—The Gospels, Acts of the Apostles, and the Epistle to the Romans. Illustrated from Ancient and Modern Authors. 6 vols. 8vo. 36s.

**GREAT TRUTHS OF THE CHRISTIAN RELIGION.** Edited by the Rev. W. U. RICHARDS. Fifth edition. 3s. cloth; or in Five Parts, wrappers, 2s. 6d.

**GRESLEY, Rev. W.**
Thoughts on Religion and Philosophy. Fcap. 8vo. 4s.
Priests and Philosophers. Fcap. 8vo. 3s. 6d.

**HEYGATE, Rev. W. E.**—Catholic Antidotes. Post 8vo., 5s. 6d.

**HOPKINS, Bishop.**—The Law of Ritualism, examined in its Relation to the Word of GOD, to the Primitive Church, to the Church of England, and to the Protestant Episcopal Church in the United States. Second edit., 2s.
A Reprint of the above, for distribution, in fcap. 8vo., 1s.

**HOSMER, Rev. A. H.**—Hearing Mass and other Customs considered. 8vo., 2s. 6d.

**HOUSMAN, Rev. H.**
Readings on the Psalms, with Notes on their Musical Treatment, originally addressed to Choristers. Fcap. 8vo., cloth, 3s. 6d.
Sermon Stories for Children's Services and Home Reading. 16mo., cl., 2s.

**HOW TO FOLLOW CHRIST**; or, Plain Words about our LORD's Life. By the Author of "Our New Life in CHRIST," &c. Fcap. 8vo., cloth, 6s. 6d., or in 12 Parts.

**HOW TO COME TO CHRIST.** By the Author of "Our New Life in CHRIST." Royal 32mo., 4d.

**HUTCHINGS, Rev. W. H.**
The Person and Work of the Holy Ghost. A Doctrinal and Devotional Treatise. Second Edition. Crown 8vo., cloth, 4s.
Some Aspects of the Cross. Second Edition. Crown 8vo., cloth, 4s.
The Life of Prayer. A Series of Lectures. Crown 8vo., cloth, 4s.

**LEA, Rev. W.**
Catechisings on the Prayer Book. Fourth edition. 18mo., cloth, 1s.
Catechisings on the Life of our LORD. 12mo., cloth, 3s. 6d.

**LESSONS FOR LITTLE CHILDREN ON THE SEASONS OF THE CHURCH.** By C. A. R. 1s.

**LESSONS FOR LITTLE CHILDREN FROM THE HISTORY OF THE CHURCH.** By C. A. R. 1s.

**LESSONS ON THE CREED.** What are we to believe. 1s. 6d.

**LIPSCOMB, Ellen.**—First Truths for the Little Ones. 18mo., cloth, 1s. 6d.

**LITTLEDALE, Rev. R. F., LL.D.**—Commentary on the Song of Songs. 12mo., antique cloth, 7s.

**LYRA SANCTORUM**; Lays for the Minor Festivals. Edited by the Rev. W. J. DEANE. 3s. 6d.

**MALAN, Rev. S. C.**
Bethany, a Pilgrimage; and Magdala, a Day by the Sea of Galilee. 1s. 6d.
The Coasts of Tyre and Sidon. A Narrative. 1s.

**MINISTRY OF CONSOLATION, The.** A Guide to Confession, for the use of Members of the Church in England. Second edition. Limp cloth, 1s. 4d.

**PAGET, REV. F. E.**—Homeward Bound; The Voyage and the Voyagers; the Pilot and the Port. Second Edition. Crown 8vo., 4s.

**PARISH AND THE PRIEST**, The. Colloquies on the Pastoral Care, and Parochial Institutions, of a Country Village. Fcap. 8vo., 2s. 6d.

**PHIPPS, Rev. J. E.**—Catechism on the Holy Scriptures. 18mo., 1s.

**READING LESSONS FROM SCRIPTURE HISTORY,** for the Use of Schools. Royal 18mo., limp cloth, 6d.

**READINGS FROM HOLY SCRIPTURE.** By the Author of "Tales of Kirkbeck." First Series, 1s. 6d.; Second Series, 2s.

**SCRIPTURE READING LESSONS FOR LITTLE CHILDREN.** With a Preface by the late Bishop Wilberforce. 2s. 6d.

**SELECTIONS, NEW AND OLD.** With a Preface by the late Bishop Wilberforce. Fcap. 8vo., 4s. 6d.

**SENTENCES** from the Works of the Author of "Amy Herbert," selected by permission. 2s.

**SPIRIT OF THE CHURCH,** The. A Selection of Articles from the *Ecclesiastic.* Post 8vo. (Pub. 7s. 6d.) *Reduced to* 3s. 6d.

**SPIRITUAL VOICES FROM THE MIDDLE AGES.** Consisting of a Selection of Abstracts from the Writings of the Fathers, adapted for the Hour of Meditation, and concluding with a Biographical Notice of their Lives. 3s. 6d.

**SUNDAY WALKS AND TALKS**; or, Conversations on the Church Services. 18mo., cloth, 1s. 6d.

**TROYTE, C. A. W.**—Change-Ringing. An Introduction to the Early Stages of the Art of Church or Hand Bell Ringing, for the Use of Beginners. Third edition. Crown 8vo., cloth, 3s. 6d.; limp, 2s. 6d. The first six chapters separately, 1s.

**WALCOTT, Rev. M. E. C.**—Cathedralia. A Constitutional History of Cathedrals of the Western Church. 8vo., 5s.

**WATSON, Rev. A.**—A Catechism on the Book of Common Prayer. 2s.

**WEST, Rev. J. R.**
A Short Treatise on the Holy Eucharist. Fcap. 8vo., 2s. 6d.
The Memorial before GOD. Crown 8vo., 9d.
Tracts on Church Principles. Cloth, 1s. 6d.
Wrawby Village Dialogues. Cloth, 1s. 6d.

## PRIVATE PRAYERS.

**AIDS TO PRAYER.** Printed on card, folded as a triptych for hanging at the bedside, with Crucifixion in centre. Price 4d., postage ½d.

**ANDREWES, Bishop.**—A Manual of Private Devotions, containing Prayers for each Day in the Week, Devotions for the Holy Communion, and for the Sick. 6d.; 9d. cloth.

**BRETT, Mr. R.**
The Churchman's Guide to Faith and Piety. A Manual of Instructions and Devotions. Fourth Edition. Cloth, 3s. 6d.; antique calf or plain morocco, 8s. 6d. 2 vols. cloth, 4s.; limp calf, 11s.; limp morocco, 12s.
Prayers for Little Children and Young Persons. 6d.; cloth, 9d.
A Manual of Devotions for School-boys. Compiled from various sources. 6d.

**CHRISTIAN SERVANT'S BOOK** of Devotion, Self-Examination, and Advice. Sixth Edition, cloth 1s.

**COSIN, Bishop.**—A Collection of Private Devotions for the Hours of Prayer. 1s.; calf, 3s. 6d.

**DEVOTIONS FOR DAILY USE.** Edited by the Hon. and Rev. C. L. Courtenay. Royal 32mo., cloth extra, 1s.

8

**DAY HOURS OF THE CHURCH OF ENGLAND,** newly Translated and Arranged according to the Prayer Book and the Authorised Translation of the Bible. 4th edition. Crown 8vo., wrapper, 1s.; cloth, 1s. 6d.; limp calf or morocco, 7s.

**SERVICE FOR CERTAIN HOLY DAYS,** The. Being a Supplement to "The Day Hours of the Church of England." Crown 8vo., 2s.

**DAY OFFICE OF THE CHURCH,** (The) according to the Kalendar of the Church of England; consisting of Lauds, Vespers, Prime, Terce, Sext, None, and Compline, throughout the Year. To which are added, the Order for the Administration of the Reserved Eucharist, Penance, and Unction; together with the Office of the Dead, Commendation of a Soul, divers Benedictions and Offices, and full Rubrical Directions.

A complete Edition, especially for Sisterhoods and Religious Houses. By the Editor of "The Little Hours of the Day." Crown 8vo., 4s. 6d.; cloth, red edges, 5s. 6d.; calf, 9s. 6d.; morocco, 10s. 6d.

**SUPPLEMENT TO THE DAY OFFICE,** 9d.

**THE OFFICE OF REPARATION TO THE BLESSED SACRAMENT**: for those who recite the Canonical Hours according to "The Day Office of the Church," "The Day Hours of the Church of England," or "Breviary Offices." Crown 8vo. 6d.

**DIAL OF MEDITATION AND PRAYER.** 2nd edition, 3d.

**GRAY, Rev. W. A.**—The Christian's Plain Guide. 32mo., cloth, 1s.; wrapper, 6d.

**HEYGATE, Rev. W. E.**
The Manual: a Book of Devotion. Eighteenth edition. Cloth limp, 1s.; boards, 1s. 3d.; roan, 1s. 6d.; cheap edition, 6d.
The Manual. Adapted for general use, 12mo., cloth, 1s. 6d.

**LITTLE HOURS OF THE DAY,** according to the Kalendar of the Church of England. 3s. 6d. cloth; 2s. 6d. wrapper.

**MALAN, Rev. S. C.**—The Pocket Book of Daily Prayers. Translated from Eastern Originals. Suited for the Waistcoat Pocket. Cloth, 6d.; roan, 1s.

**THE ORDER FOR PRIME, TERCE, SEXT, NONE, AND COMPLINE, ACCORDING TO THE USE OF THE CHURCH OF ENGLAND.** Newly revised. Price 9d. in wrapper.

This is printed in a form suitable for binding with the various editions of the Prayer Book from 24mo. to crown 8vo.

**PAGET, Rev. F. E.**—Sursum Corda: Aids to Private Devotion. Collected from the Writings of English Churchmen. 2s. 6d. cloth.

**PATHWAY OF FAITH,** The, or a Manual of Instructions and Prayers. For the use of those who desire to serve God in the station of life in which He has placed them. Limp cloth, 1s.; cloth boards, 1s. 3d.

**PIOUS CHURCHMAN,** The: a Manual of Devotion and Spiritual Instruction. 1s. 6d.

**POCKET MANUAL OF PRAYERS FOR THE HOURS.** 6d. Cloth, with the Collects, 1s.

**POLLOCK, Rev. J. S.**
Resting Places. A Manual of Christian Doctrine, Duty, and Devotion, for Private and Family Use. Third edition, revised. Imperial 32mo. limp cloth, 1s. 6d.; cloth boards, 2s.
The Plain Guide. 44th thousand. Super-royal 32mo., 3d.; limp cloth, 6d.; cloth boards, 9d.

**PRAYERS FOR THE SEVEN CANONICAL HOURS,** together with Devotions, Acts of Contrition, Faith, Hope, and Love. 32mo. cloth, 1s.

**PRIMER,** (The) set forth at large with many Godly and Devout Prayers. Edited, from the Post-Reformation Recension, by the Rev. Gerard Moultrie, M.A., Vicar of South Leigh. 4th Thousand. 18mo., cloth, 3s.
THE PRIMER, printed on toned paper and rubricated, 18mo., antique cloth 5s.
THE HOURS OF THE PRIMER, Published separately for the use of individual members of a household in Family Prayer. 18mo., cloth, 1s.
HORARIUM; seu Libellus Precationum, Latinè editus. 18mo., cloth, 1s.

**SMITH, Rev. T. F.**— The Devout Chorister. Thoughts on his Vocation, and a Manual of Devotions for his use. Fifth Edition, 32mo., cloth, 1s.

**YOUNG CHURCHMAN'S MANUAL,** The. Second edition. 6d.

## FAMILY PRAYERS.

**BOOK OF FAMILY PRAYERS,** collected from the Public Liturgy of the Church of England. By the Sacrist of Durham. 2s.

**BOWDLER, Rev. T.**—Prayers for a Christian Household, chiefly taken from the Scriptures, from the Ancient Liturgies, and the Book of Common Prayer. Fcap. 8vo., cloth, 2s. 6d.

**CARTER, Rev. T. T.**— Family Prayers. 4th edition. Cloth, 1s.

**DOMESTIC OFFICES:** being Morning and Evening Prayer for the Use of Families. Wrapper, 6d. ; cloth, 8d.

**FAMILY DEVOTIONS FOR A FORTNIGHT.** Compiled from the Works of BISHOP ANDREWES, KEN, WILSON, KETTLEWELL, NELSON, SPINCKES, &c. (Suited also for private use.) New Edition, Fcap. 8vo., cloth, 1s. 6d.

**FAMILY PRAYERS FOR THE CHILDREN OF THE CHURCH.** 4d., cloth 6d.

**FAMILY PRAYERS FOR THE CHRISTIAN YEAR,** together with Collects, with Versicles and Responses. 1s. 2d. wrapper, 1s. 6d. roan.

**MONSELL.**—Prayers and Litanies, taken from Holy Scripture ; together with a Calendar and table of Lessons. Arranged by the Rev. J. S. B. Monsell, LL.D. 16mo., cloth, 1s.

**SHORT SERVICES FOR DAILY USE IN FAMILIES.** Cloth, 1s.

**SUCKLING, Rev. R. A.**—Family Prayers adapted to the course of the Ecclesiastical Year. 6d. ; cloth, 1s.

## FOR THE SICK AND AFFLICTED.

**BRETT, Mr. R.**
Devotions for the Sick Room, Prayers in Sickness, &c. Cloth, 2s. 6d.
Companion for the Sick Room : being a Compendium of Christian Doctrine. 2s. 6d. These two bound together in 1 vol. cloth, price 5s.
Offices for the Sick and Dying. Reprinted from the above. 1s.
Leaflets for the Sick and Dying; supplementary to the Offices for the same in "The Churchman's Guide to Faith and Piety." First Series. Price per set of eight, 6d., cardboard, 9d.
Instructions, Prayers, and Holy Aspirations for the Sick Room. 4d., cloth 6d.

**BROWN, Rev. R. C. L.**—The Dead in CHRIST. A Word of Consolation to Mourners. Super-royal 32mo., cloth, 1s. 6d.

**MANUAL FOR MOURNERS,** with Devotions, Directions, and Forms of Self-Examination. Fcap. 8vo., 2s. 6d.

**POCKET BOOK OF DEVOTIONS AND EXTRACTS FOR INVALIDS.** By C. L. Edited by the Ven. ALFRED POTT, B.D., Archdeacon of Berkshire, Vicar of Clifton Hampden. Super royal 32mo., cloth, 1s. 6d.

**PRAYERS AND MAXIMS,** in large type, 2s. 6d.

**WILKINSON, Rev. J. B.**—The Hour of Death. A Manual of Prayers and Meditations intended chiefly for those in Sorrow or in Sickness. Royal 32mo., 2s.

## EUCHARISTIC MANUALS.

**AN ALTAR BOOK FOR YOUNG PERSONS.** Suitable also for Choristers. Cloth, with a picture of the Crucifixion, 8d.; with 9 pictures, 1s. 3d.; do. red edges, gold lettered, 1s. 6d.

**DEVOTIONS FOR HOLY COMMUNION.** Edited by the Rev. W. U. Richards. 32mo., cloth, 1s.

**EUCHARISTIC DEVOTIONS,** with Preparations and Thanksgivings for Young Persons Unconfirmed or not Communicating. Royal 32mo., cloth, 9d. A companion book to "The Devout Chorister," and may be had bound with it, 1s. 6d. cloth.

**GUIDE TO THE EUCHARIST.** Containing Instructions and Directions with Forms of Preparation and Self-Examination. 4d.

**HOLY EUCHARIST,** The. A Manual containing Directions and suitable Devotions for those who remain in Church but do not Communicate. By a Parish Priest. 6d.

**MALAN, Rev. S. C.**
Prayers and Thanksgivings for the Holy Communion, chiefly for the use of the Clergy. Translated from Coptic, Armenian, and other Eastern Rituals. 1s. 6d. cloth.
Preparation for Holy Communion of the Body and Blood of CHRIST, with Prayers and Thanksgivings for the same; chiefly for the use of the Laity. Gathered and translated from Armenian and other Eastern Originals. 1s. 6d. cloth.

**MANUAL FOR COMMUNICANTS:** being an Assistant to a Devout and Worthy Reception of the LORD's Supper. Roan, 1s.; paper cover, 6d. In large type, 6d.

**PRYNNE, Rev. G. R.**—Eucharistic Manual, consisting of Instructions and Devotions for the Holy Sacrament of the Altar. From various sources. 1s. 6d., cloth; calf, 4s. 6d.; morocco, 5s. Cheap edition, limp cloth, 1s.; roan, 2s. 6d.

**SCUDAMORE, Rev. W. E.**
Steps to the Altar: a Manual of Devotion for the Blessed Eucharist. 55th edition. Royal 32mo., cloth, 2s.; calf or morocco, 4s. 6d. Demy 18mo., cloth, 1s.; calf or morocco, 3s. 6d.; roan, 2s. 6d. Imperial 32mo., cloth, 6d. Imitation morocco, 1s. 3d.
Incense for the Altar. A Series of Devotions for the Use of earnest Communicants, whether they receive frequently or at longer intervals. Royal 32mo., cloth, 2s. 6d.; limp calf, 5s.

**SHIPLEY, Rev. O.**
The Divine Liturgy. A Manual of Devotions for the Sacrament of the Altar. Fourth Edition. Limp cloth, 1s. 6d. Superior Edition, cloth boards, 2s. 6d.
The Daily Sacrifice: a Manual of Spiritual Communion. From Ancient Sources. Limp cloth, 1s.; cloth extra, 1s. 6d.

# DEVOTIONAL BOOKS.

**BELLARMINE.**—The Seven Words from the Cross. A Devotional Commentary. By Bellarmine. Second edition. 1s. 6d.

**BRETT, Mr. R.**
Reflections, Meditations, and Prayers, on the Holy Life and Passion of our LORD. New edition, 5s.
Fervent Aspirations after Divine Love and Thanksgivings on the Passion. Cloth 8d., wrapper, 6d.

**COMMUNION WITH GOD.** Meditations and Prayers for One Week. By a Clergyman. Fcap. 8vo., cloth, 2s.

**DIVINE MASTER, The:** a Devotional Manual illustrating the Way of the Cross. With Ten Steel Engravings. 9th edition, 2s. 6d.; morocco 5s.; antique calf or morocco 7s. Cheap edition in wrapper, 1s.

**HELPS TO MEDITATION FOR BEGINNERS.** By a Priest of the Church of England. Edited by the Rev. GEORGE BODY. 18mo. 3d.

**HEYGATE, Rev. W. E.**—The Wedding Gift. A Devotional Manual for the Married, or those intending to Marry. 2nd edition, revised and enlarged. 3s.

**A FEW DEVOTIONAL HELPS FOR THE CHRISTIAN SEASONS.** Royal 32mo. 2 Vols., cloth 5s. 6d.

**HIDDEN LIFE, The.** Translated from Nepveu's Pensées Chrétiennes. 3rd edition, enlarged. 18mo. 2s.

**HOLY CHILD JESUS.** Thoughts and Prayers on the Holy Infancy and Childhood of our Blessed LORD and SAVIOUR, JESUS CHRIST. With 8 Engravings. 1s. 6d. cloth; 1s. wrapper; morocco, 4s.

**HOLY CHILDHOOD OF OUR BLESSED LORD.** Meditations for a Month. By the Author of "Tales of Kirkbeck." 6d.

**THE KALENDAR OF THE IMITATION:** Sentences for every day of the year from the "Imitatio Christi." Translated from the edition of 1630. Edited by the late Rev. J. M. NEALE, D.D. New edition, royal 32mo., cloth, 1s.

**KEMPIS.**—The Soliloquy of the Soul, and the Garden of Roses. Translated from Thomas à Kempis. By the Rev. W. B. FLOWER, B.A. 2s.; cheap edition, 1s.

**MALAN, Rev. S. C.**
Meditations on our LORD's Passion. Translated from the Armenian of Matthew, Vartabed. 2s. 6d.
Companion for Lent. Being an Exhortation to Repentance, from the Syriac of S. Ephraem; and Thoughts for every Day in Lent, gathered from other Eastern Fathers and Divines. 1s. 3d.

**MISERERE:** the Fifty-first Psalm. With Devotional Notes. Reprinted from Neale's "Commentary on the Psalms." With additions by the Rev. R. F. LITTLEDALE, LL.D. 6d.; cloth, 1s.

**MOULTRIE, Rev. G.**
Hymns and Lyrics, for the Seasons and Saints' Days of the Church. Fcap. 8vo., 2s. 6d.
Offices for Holy Week and Easter, after the Primer Use, together with the Meditations on the Life and Passion of our LORD. Edited by the Rev. G. MOULTRIE, M.A. 18mo. 3s.

**OUR NEW LIFE IN CHRIST.** Edited by a Parish Priest, C. L. C. Fourth edition. 18mo., cloth, 1s.; cheap edition, 6d.

**A SEQUEL TO "OUR NEW LIFE IN CHRIST;" OR, THE PRESENCE OF JESUS ON THE ALTAR.** With a Few Simple Ways of Worshipping Him at the Celebration of the Blessed Sacrament. To which are added, Devotions and Hymns. 18mo., limp cloth, 1s.; cloth boards, red edges, 1s. 6d.

12

**PAGET, Rev. F. E.**—The Christian's Day. Royal 32mo., 2s. cloth.

**PEOPLE'S HYMNAL,** The, containing 600 Hymns, Carols, and Metrical Litanies. Wrapper, 6d.; limp cloth, 8d.; cloth boards, red edges, 1s.; roan, red edges, 1s. 9d. Large Type edition, cloth boards, 2s.; roan, 4s.

**PRACTICAL SCIENCE OF THE CROSS IN THE USE OF THE SACRAMENTS OF PENANCE AND THE EUCHARIST.** By M. the Abbé Grou. Translated from the French. 18mo., cloth, 2s. 6d.

**PRACTICE OF THE PRESENCE OF GOD THE BEST RULE OF A HOLY LIFE,** being Conversations and Letters of Brother Lawrence. Sixth edition. Royal 32mo, 4d.; cloth, 6d.; morocco, 1s. 6d.

**PSALTER,** The; or Seven Ordinary Hours of Prayer, according to the use of the Church of Sarum. Beautifully printed and bound in antique parchment. Reduced to 15s.

**SHIPLEY, The Rev. Orby.**
Eucharistic Meditations for a Month on the Most Holy Communion. Translated from the French of Avrillon. Limp cloth, 2s. 6d.
Daily Meditations: from Ancient Sources. Edited by the Rev. Orby Shipley. Advent to Easter. Cloth, 1s. 6d.
Daily Meditations for a Month, on some of the more moving truths of Christianity; in order to determine the Soul to be in earnest in the love and service of her God. From ancient sources. Edited by the Rev. Orby Shipley. Cloth, 1s.
A Treatise of the Virtue of Humility, abridged from the Spanish of Rodriguez; for the use of persons living in the world. Cloth, 1s.
Considerations on Mysteries of the Faith, newly translated and abridged from the Original Spanish of Luis de Granada. 2s. cloth.
Spiritual Exercises: Readings for a Retreat of Seven Days. Translated and abridged from the French of Bourdaloue. Edited by the Rev. Orby Shipley. 1s. 6d.

**THREE HOURS AGONY** : Meditations, Prayers, and Hymns on the Seven Words from the Cross of our Most Holy Redeemer, together with Additional Devotions on the Passion. Fourteenth Thousand. 4d.

**TUTE, Rev. J. S.**—Meditations on the Most Precious Blood and Example of Christ. Fcap. 8vo., cloth, 1s. 6d.

**VERSES FOR THE SUNDAYS AND HOLIDAYS OF THE CHRISTIAN YEAR.** By the Author of the " Daily Life of the Christian Child," &c., with Illustrations. 2s.

**WILLIAMS, The late Rev. I.**
The Altar; or Meditations in Verse on the Holy Communion. By the author of " The Cathedral." 2s. 6d.
Hymns on the Catechism. 6d., cloth 1s.

**WOODHOUSE, Rev. F. C.**—The Exemplar of Penitence. Meditations on the Fifty-first Psalm, for the Sundays in Lent and at other times. Crown 8vo., 1s. 6d.

## BOOKS FOR THE USE OF THE CLERGY.

**THE PRIEST'S PRAYER BOOK,** with a brief Pontifical. Containing Private Prayers and Intercessions; Offices, Readings, Prayers, Litanies, and Hymns, for the Visitation of the Sick ; Offices for Bible and Confirmation Classes, Cottage Lectures, &c.; Notes on Confession, Direction, Missions, and Retreats; Remedies for Sin; Anglican Orders; Bibliotheca Sacerdotalis, &c., &c. Fifth Edition, much enlarged.

|  | s. | d. |  | s. | d. |
|---|---|---|---|---|---|
| One vol. cloth...... | 6 | 6 | Two vols. cloth .... | 7 | 6 |
| Calf or morocco.... | 10 | 6 | Calf or morocco.... | 15 | 0 |
| With Common Prayer, 2s. 6d. additional. | | | | | |

**THE CLERGYMAN'S MANUAL OF PRIVATE PRAYERS.** Collected and Compiled from Various Sources. A Companion Book to "The Priest's Prayer Book." Cloth, 1s.

**HORARIUM;** seu Libellus Precationum, Latinè editus. 18mo., cloth, 1s.

**MEMORIALE VITÆ SACERDOTALIS;** or, Solemn Warnings of the Great Shepherd, JESUS CHRIST, to the Clergy of His Holy Church. From the Latin of Arvisenet. Adapted to the Use of the English Church by the BISHOP OF BRECHIN. Second edition. Fcap. 8vo., cloth, 3s. 6d.

**THE PRIEST IN HIS INNER LIFE.** By H. P. L. 1s.

**HEYGATE, Rev. W. E.**—Ember Hours. New edition, revised, with an Essay on RELIGION IN RELATION TO SCIENCE, by the Rev. T. S. ACKLAND, M.A., Vicar of Balne, author of "Story of Creation," &c. Fcap. 8vo., cloth, 3s.

**THE ORDER FOR A CHILDREN'S SERVICE.** With Music. Price 3d., cloth 4d. Published with the approval of the Archbishops of Canterbury and Dublin, and authorized for use in the Dioceses of Winchester, Ely, Peterborough, Lincoln, Bath and Wells, and Oxford.

**OWEN, Rev. R.**—An Introduction to the Study of Dogmatic Theology. 8vo., 12s.

**PAGET, Rev. F. E.**
Memoranda Parochialia; or, the Parish Priest's Pocket Book. 3s. 6d.; double size 5s.
Sermons for Special Occasions. Containing Twenty-one Sermons for Consecration of Churches, Churchyards, Restoration, Anniversary, Foundation Stone, New School, School Feast, Confirmation, Ordination, Visitation, Church and Educational Societies, Choirs, Wakes, Festivals, Clubs, and Assizes. Post 8vo., 5s.

**SERMONS REGISTER,** for Ten Years, by which an account may be kept of Sermons, the number, subject, and when preached. Post 4to., 1s.

**REGISTER OF SERMONS, PREACHERS, NUMBER OF COMMUNICANTS, AND AMOUNT OF OFFERTORY.** Fcap. 4to., roan, 4s. 6d. (The Book of Strange Preachers as ordered by the 52nd Canon.)

**REGISTER OF PERSONS CONFIRMED AND ADMITTED TO HOLY COMMUNION.** For 500 names, 4s. 6d. For 1000 names, 7s. 6d., half-bound.

**THE LITANY** from the Book of Common Prayer, together with the latter part of the COMMINATION SERVICE, with Musical Notation throughout for Priest, Choir, and People. Edited by RICHARD REDHEAD. Demy 4to. Handsomely printed in red and black. Wrapper, 7s. 6d.; imitation morocco, 18s.; morocco plain, 24s.; morocco panelled, &c., 30s.

**THOMPSON, Rev. H.**
Concionalia; Outlines of Sermons for Parochial Use throughout the Year. First Series. Third edition. Fcap. 8vo., 7s. 6d.
Concionalia. Second Series. Fcap. 8vo., 6s. 6d.

**BARING GOULD, Rev. S.**
One Hundred Sketches of Sermons for Extempore Preachers. Third Edition. Crown 8vo., 6s.
Village Conferences on the Creed. Crown 8vo., 3s. 6d.

14                                            [*J. Masters & Co.,*

# SERMONS AND LECTURES.

**ASHLEY, Rev. J. M.**
The Victory of the Spirit: a Course of Short Sermons by way of Commentary on the Eighth Chapter of S. Paul's Epistle to the Romans. Fcap. 8vo., cloth, 2s.
Thirteen Sermons from the Quaresimale of Quirico Rossi. Translated from the Italian. Edited by J. M. ASHLEY, B.C.L. Fcap. 8vo., cloth, 3s. 6d.

**BAINES, Rev. J.**—Sermons. Fcap. 8vo. cloth, 5s.

**BRIGHT, Rev. Canon, D.D.**—Eighteen Sermons of S. Leo the Great on the Incarnation, translated with Notes and with the "Tome" of S. Leo in the original. 8vo., cloth, 5s.

**BUTLER, Rev. W. J.**—Sermons for Working Men. Second edition. 12mo., 6s. 6d.

**CHAMBERS, Rev. J. C.**—Fifty-two Sermons for the Seasons of the Church. 8vo., 6s.

**CHAMBERLAIN, Rev. T.**
The Theory of Christian Worship. Second edition. 3s. 6d.
The Seven Ages of the Church as indicated in the Messages to the Seven Churches of Asia. Post 8vo., 2s.

**CHANTER, Rev. J. M.**—Sermons. 12mo., 3s. 6d.

**CODD, Rev. E. T.**—Sermons addressed to a Country Congregation, including Four preached before the University of Cambridge. Third Series. 12mo., 6s. 6d.

**DAVIES, Rev. G.**—Benefit Club Sermons. 1st and 2nd Series. In one Vol. Second edition. 4to., 3s.

**EVANS, Rev. A. B., D.D.**—Christianity in its Homely Aspects: Sermons on Various Subjects. Second Series. 12mo., 3s.

**FLOWER, Rev. W. B.**—Sermons for the Seasons of the Church, translated from S. Bernard. 8vo., 6s.

**FORD, Rev. J.**—Sermons from the Quaresimale of P. Paolo Segneri. 8vo., 3 vols. 6s. each.

**FREEMAN, Archdeacon.**—Four Sermons for the Season of Advent. Post 8vo., 2s.

**GALTON, Rev. J. L.**
One Hundred and Forty-two Lectures on the Book of Revelation. In Two Vols. Fcap. 8vo., 18s.
Notes of Lectures on the Book of Canticles or Song of Solomon, delivered in the Parish Church of S. Sidwell, Exeter. 6s.

**GRESLEY, Rev. W.**
Practical Sermons. 12mo., 3s. 6d.
Sermons preached at Brighton. 12mo., 3s. 6d.

**HAMILTON, Rev. L. R.**—Parochial Sermons. Fcap. 8vo., 3s. 6d.

**IRONS, Rev. W. J., D.D.**
The Preaching of CHRIST. A Series of Sixty Sermons for the People. In a packet, 5s., cloth, 6s.
The Miracles of CHRIST: being a Second Series of Sermons for the People. Second edition. 8vo., 6s.

**LEA, Rev. W.**—Sermons on the Prayer Book. Fcap. 8vo., 2s.

**LEE, Rev. F. G., D.C.L.**
Miscellaneous Sermons, by Clergymen of the Church of England. Edited by F. G. Lee. Crown 8vo., 3s. 6d.
The Message of Reconciliation. In Four Sermons. 8vo., 2s.

**MILLARD, Rev. F. M.**—S. Peter's Denial of Christ. Seven short Sermons to Boys. Fcap. 8vo., 1s. 4d.

**NEWLAND, Rev. H.**—Postils; Short Sermons on the Parables, &c., adapted from the Fathers. Second edition. Fcap. 8vo., 3s.

**NUGEE, Rev. G.**—The Words from the Cross as applied to our own Deathbeds. Second edition. Fcap. 8vo., 2s. 6d.

**PAGET, Rev. F. E.**
Sermons on the Saints' Days. 12mo., 3s. 6d.
Sermons for Special Occasions. Crown 8vo., 5s.

**PHILARET (Metropolitan of Moscow).**—Select Sermons. Translated from the Russian. Crown 8vo., 6s. 6d.

**PRICHARD, Rev. J. C.**—Sermons. Fcap. 8vo., 4s. 6d.

**PRYNNE, Rev. G. R.**
Plain Parochial Sermons. Second Series. 8vo., 10s. 6d.
Parochial Sermons. (New Volume.) 8vo. cloth, 10s. 6d.

**POTT, The Ven. Archdeacon.**
Confirmation Lectures delivered to a Village Congregation in the Diocese of Oxford. Third edition. 2s.
Village Lectures on the Sacraments and Occasional Services of the Church. 2s.

**SERMONS** by various Contributors illustrating the Offices of the Prayer Book. 8vo., 3s. 6d.

**STRETTON, Rev. H.**—The Acts of S. Mary Magdalene considered in Sixteen Sermons. 8vo., 5s.

**SUCKLING, Rev. R. A.**—Sermons Plain and Practical. Fourth edit. Fcap. 8vo., 3s. 6d.

**VERNON, Rev. J. E.**—Bible Truths in Simple Words. Short Addresses to Children. Fcap. 8vo., 3s.

**WEST, Rev. J. R.**
Sermons on the Ascension of our Lord. Fcap. 8vo., 3s. 6d.
Parish Sermons for the Advent and Christmas Seasons. Fcap. 8vo. 3s.
Parish Sermons on the Holy Eucharist. Fcap. 8vo., 4s. 6d.

**WILKINSON, Rev. J. B.**
Mission Sermons. Twenty-five Plain Sermons preached in London and Country Churches and Missions. Second edition. Fcap. 8vo., 3s. 6d.
Mission Sermons. Second Series. Fcap. 8vo., 5s.
Mission Sermons. Third Series. Fcap. 8vo., 6s.

**WINDSOR, Rev. S. B.**—Sermons for Soldiers preached at Home and Abroad. Fcap. 8vo., 3s. 6d.

**WROTH, Rev. W. R.**—Five Sermons on some of the Old Testament Types of Holy Baptism. Post 8vo., 3s.

J. MASTERS AND CO., 78, NEW BOND STREET

www.ingramcontent.com/pod-product-compliance
Lightning Source LLC
Chambersburg PA
CBHW020619030726
47497CB00007B/2321